Rose
and the
Wicked Wizard

Other Books in the Rose Iris Adventure Series:

Rose Iris and the Enchanted Stones.

Rose Iris and the Rock Trolls.

Rose Iris and the Wicked Wizard

BARBARA HOPKINS

THE CHOIR PRESS

This edition published in 2021 by The Choir Press

ISBN 978-1-78963-222-4

Contents

For my dearest daughters, Loraine and Yvonne. Many a time I would bring them home from nursery-school to a freezing cold flat. We would sit on the rug by the warm-air central heating vent and listen to the tiny little man who lived inside, as he cranked up the mechanisms, which turned the cogs and started the boiler, before the fan would begin to blow and warm our fingers and toes.

Thanks to my dear husband, Barry, for his help, advice and patience throughout.

Illustrations by the author
Medium predominantly ball-point pen

Another Adventure Begins

Rose Iris had only just woken up, and was lying in bed listening to Bert the wood pigeon as he continued to complain to her about his toe bleeding, when her bedroom door burst open and her mother's smiling face appeared.

"White rabbits," her mother called. "Rise and shine."

"White rabbits," the little girl replied as she jumped out of bed and slid her feet into her pretty pink slippers.

Now you might think that maybe there were white rabbits on the lawn outside her house, and she would quickly run to the window to see them, but you would be mistaken. On the first day of each month, before they spoke any other words to each other at all, her parents would say, "White rabbits." Then one of them would hurry to Rose Iris's bedroom, pop their head around the door and say, "White rabbits," often before the little girl was fully awake. It was supposed to bring good luck into the house for a whole month, and since today was the first of August, these words had to be spoken before any others.

Rose Iris wondered how her parents could always remember to say the lucky words. She herself was a chatterbox and often would forget that it was a new month. As soon as she awoke, she would begin to chatter.

"Oh dear, what a pity, this will not be a lucky month," her parents would complain jokingly.

The little girl washed her face, got dressed and went downstairs. Breakfast, her favourite cereal, was already on the table. Her father was reading the newspaper by this time. Only the hair on the top of his head poked up above the large Sunday paper, and four fingers of each hand protruded around the sides, as he held it high and wide in front of him. Rose Iris preferred her father to be reading week-day papers. They were very much smaller, and he would hold them lower. She loved to watch his face and his lips moving very slightly, even though no sound came from his mouth because he was reading underneath his breath.

Her mother struggled to feed Rose Iris's baby brother, who sat gurgling in his highchair. For each spoonful of food that went into his mouth, three quarters of a spoonful come back out, accompanied by a cluster of frothy bubbles, since he insisted on blowing raspberries at the same time as he ate his breakfast.

Suddenly, her father's head and eyes appeared from around the side of the newspaper. "It says here that the Emperor of China's daughter, Princess Mae Woo, has disappeared. It is thought that she may have been kidnapped, but nobody has a clue as to who has taken her or where she may be. Her parents are broken hearted," he said in a very concerned voice.

"How terrible. I don't know what I would do if either of my two little horrors were taken away. I hope they find her very soon," her mother replied.

Rose Iris felt very sorry for the emperor and his daughter, but she was in a hurry to go out to play in the park with her friends. She finished eating her breakfast, ran upstairs and cleaned her teeth before asking her mother to brush and plait her hair, then she went back to tidy her bedroom. She put all her toys away into the special box that her father had made for her to keep them in. There was only one toy that never went into the box and that was her favourite rag doll. Daisy was her special friend and was allowed to lie on Rose Iris's bed in the daytime and sleep with her at night-time.

"I won't be long, Daisy." She gave the doll a hug and a kiss as she spoke, then carefully placed her on a chair until her mother made the bed later that morning. Then she ran back downstairs.

"Bye! See you later," she called to her parents as she walked out of the front door, slamming it loudly behind her. The park was exactly opposite her house so she knew they wouldn't worry.

It was only two weeks since her last adventure into the magical world and she could think of little else but what had happened whilst she was there.

As she strolled through the park gate, she saw that none of her friends had yet arrived. She wondered when Leanora would return needing her help.

Well! she didn't have to wait for very long at all, because as she walked along admiring the flowers and listening to Bert still complaining, she noticed in the distance a small figure, and as the person came closer and became larger she realised that it was her dear friend Leanora. Even before the sound of the clinking and clanking pots and pans that the old woman always kept hanging on the handle of her pram reached her ears, Rose Iris started to run towards the old Gypsy.

When she reached Leanora, she threw her arms around her and hugged her very tightly.

"Why did you leave without saying a proper good-bye and giving me a hug?" she asked excitedly. "Have you come to take me on another journey into the magical world?"

ROSE IRIS

"One question at a time," said the old Gypsy. "First, I am sorry to have vanished as I did, but I had received a whispered message on the breeze. It was from Orgon, the magic maker and wise man of the mud fairies. He was begging me to go to him as he needed my help. It was most upsetting having to leave you in this world, but I knew you could not accompany me, or your parents would have been worrying. Secondly, yes, I do need your help. We have to find the Emperor of China's daughter. Her father is sick and will not eat or drink and so his body is wasting to bones," she continued.

"Shall I go home and get the tin with cashews written on it, so you can use it to keep the enchanted stones in?" Rose Iris was delighted to know that she was going on another adventure.

"No, there is no time, child, for if we do not find the princess soon, the poor emperor will die of a broken heart," said Leanora.

"Does that mean that I will not have to become tiny again?" the little girl asked excitedly.

"I'm afraid you will, but so long as you have the enchanted stones in your pretty locket, we can use them together with a new magic potion that I have learnt to make, which has the power to shrink you," the old Gypsy replied. "Without the tin we will have nowhere to keep the enchanted stones, so you will need to give me your locket and I will wear it around my wrist. As you know it will break if it shrinks with you and the stones do not. When we have saved the princess, I will return the locket to you undamaged, I promise," she continued.

"Oh, by the way, have you noticed something different

about me?" As she spoke the old Gypsy walked up and down in a very odd manner. She was trying to look elegant as she swayed back and forth along the path. Unfortunately, it was more of a plod than an elegant stride. Then she spun around and stood still with her arms akimbo (that means with her elbows out to the side and her hands on her hips). "Ta-da," she said, as she waited for the little girl to reply.

"Umm," Rose Iris tilted her head to one side and held her hand to her chin, as she pretended to think deeply.

Leanora spun around once more. All the while she had a most unusual grin on her face. "Ta-da," she repeated.

"Humm," the little girl teased.

"Oh! for goodness sake. Whatever is wrong with your eyes child?" The old Gypsy was beginning to lose her patience.

"Of course, I can see what is different. You are not wearing your trousers under your skirt," the little girl replied.

"No, that's not it. What else has changed?" Once more the old Gypsy spun around and stood with her hands on her hips.

"Oh! I know. It's your cardigan. You have a new one. I was only joking with you." Rose Iris giggled as she spoke. "It really is very much better than your old one. Where did you get it?"

"Do you remember my dear friend Dolly, who lives on the farm?" Leanora replied. "We were enjoying a wee sip of CIDER and getting very merry. Well! it might have been a little more than a wee sip. To be honest, quite a lot more than a sip. Anyway, her cat saw a hanging woollen thread on my beautiful blue cardigan sleeve and caught hold of it. He ran around and around the room with the thread attached to his claw, all the time getting more and more tangled in it.

Gradually all the stitches came undone, until at last the whole sleeve disappeared. So, when I left the farm the next morning Dolly gave me one of her cardigans, as well as the usual loaf of bread, some packets of tea and some matches for making my fires to cook on. Now, we have no time to waste. If you have the stones in your locket, pass it to me. If you don't have them, oh dear, we are surely lost."

"I do have them. You know I never take them out of my locket." As she spoke Rose Iris removed the golden chain, from which hung the oval locket containing a picture of her grandmother, and the three enchanted stones, tied together with Ilani the mud fairy's pink, plaited hair, and passed it to Leanora.

The old Gypsy wrapped it twice around her wrist and Rose Iris did up the clasp that joined the two ends of the chain together. Then, Leanora slipped her hand into her new red cardigan pocket and pulled out a small bottle with a screw lid. She removed the lid and whispered these magic words.

"Licondo, liberata caziendo."

Immediately a waft of silvery smoke floated out from the opening in the neck of the bottle. It wriggled for a few seconds in the air, then shot towards Rose Iris and straight up her nose. She sneezed once, twice, three times, before starting to shiver all over. After several seconds, as on her previous visits to the other world, she began to shrink. Gradually she became smaller and smaller, tinier and tinier until she could hardly be seen amongst the blades of grass. She was not at all surprised since she was getting quite used to this happening. It had already happened twice before.

"Do you want to go into the old pram, or would you rather travel on my beautiful felt hat, dear?" Leanora bent down and lifted the tiny girl up from amongst the blades of grass as she spoke.

"Oh! I'd much rather travel on your hat," the little girl replied. "Every time I see you it looks even more beautiful than the last time."

The Gypsy placed Rose Iris on the hat in a safe position near the hatband, so she would have something to hold on to if she were to lose her balance. Then they started their journey.

"Do you know where Princess Mae Woo is, Leanora?" the tiny girl asked.

"No, we will have to see if anyone else has heard where she may be. Wherever she is, I am sure it will be a long distance from here and there may be many dangers on our journey, but I have the enchanted stones in your locket fixed safely around my wrist, so hopefully we will not meet too many problems," her friend replied. "I think the best place to start is to find Miss Nosey Nora. If anyone knows anything at all it will be her."

"Who is Nosey Nora?" the little girl asked.

"She's a very good friend of mine, but whatever you do don't discuss anything you don't want the whole world to know about when we meet her," the old Gypsy replied.

LEANORA

Finding Miss Nosey Nora

They began their journey right away, since there was no time to waste. Rose Iris felt excited to be going on another adventure with her Gypsy friend who, I forgot to tell you, was also a witch.

"First we must find Nosey Nora," said Leanora. "I am sure she will be able to tell us where we can find Princess Mae Woo."

"What a lovely name the princess has," the little girl replied.

"Yes, the name means beautiful lake, and it suits the princess well, since she is not only beautiful on the outside, but also gentle, placid, kind and generous on the inside," the old Gypsy replied.

Leanora walked for a very long time with the pots and pans jingling and jangling on the handle of the old pram and Rose Iris clinging tightly to the hatband. At first, they neither saw nor heard a single soul, but then suddenly, as they travelled along a leafy lane, they heard a terrible commotion on the other side of a hedge that surrounded a grassy meadow, and loud voices could be heard arguing.

"Just leave me alone," it was a very posh lady's voice. "I don't want you to keep bothering me. I just want to sit on a grassy bank and eat some clover in peace, then have a little sleep. Why won't you just go away?"

"It's only because I like you so much and that I want to be your friend," said a second, much deeper voice.

"Yes, I know you like me, you keep telling me so, but I'm

not in the mood to be friendly. I told you, I just want to be alone," said the first voice.

"You're a most unfriendly creature," said the other voice angrily. "I don't know why I waste my time speaking to you. You're much too stuck up."

"That's it. Put up your paws. I've had enough of this," the lady replied.

Then there followed the sound of a fight going on. First a thump, then a biff, followed by another thump, then a bop.

Leanora bent forward and carefully put the brake on the old pram. Then she slowly pushed open the large, heavy gate that closed the meadow off from the lane and popped her head around the hedge. "Whatever is going on? What's all this noise?" she asked. Then she recognised the culprits. It was Gilliad the hare and a young lady hare called Giselle. They were both wearing boxing gloves and taking wild punches at each other.

"He won't leave me alone. I've had a very busy morning eating clover and sleeping, so now all I want is to enjoy a snack and have a little rest on a leafy bank," said the lady hare, lowering her boxing gloves as she spoke.

"Well! she's so unfriendly, I only want to make her acquaintance, but she keeps punching me on the nose and saying she's not interested in me," said Gilliad.

"Why don't you wait until Giselle is in a more friendly mood? Then I am sure she will be happy to be your friend," said Leanora. "I wonder, do either of you know where Nosey Nora is?" she continued.

"I don't, but I did see her about two days ago. She was heading north, so I guess that would be the best direction to

GILLIAD AND GISELLE

head for," Gilliad replied as he received a very hard thump on the nose that sent him reeling backwards.

"I saw Bramble Bottom yesterday and he said he had seen her at the crossroads between Much Cowarne and Little Frome," Giselle said, just before receiving a sly thump on the jaw. For a moment, her jaw went all wonky, but she used her own boxing glove to push it back straight, then wriggled it a few times to make sure it was in the proper place, before giving Gilliad another wallop on the nose, followed by a clout around the ear.

"Then I suppose that is the best place to begin." Leanora was glad that they now had a clue as to which direction Nosey Nora was heading. "Thank you for your help," she said.

"What's that funny thing on your hat?" Giselle asked.

"Oh! That's my dear friend Rose Iris. Maybe, when you are in a more friendly mood, you would like to meet her," said the old Gypsy.

"I have already met her," said Gilliad in a rather snooty voice. "As a matter of fact, she is my friend too. She's a much nicer person than you. I am surprised that you haven't heard how brave she was, saving all the local folk from Queen Elvira and her rock trolls."

"Of course, I've heard of Rose Iris, but I just haven't met her before," said Giselle.

Just at that moment Gilliad got an itch on his bottom. He tried to scratch it but could not, for his boxing gloves got in the way. Then the fur on his back began to move from side to side before standing on end. Two little heads popped out from amongst the fur. One wore a beautiful blue cavalier's hat whilst the second simply smiled, fluttered her eyelashes and looked adoringly at the other. It was Captain Dandy and Edwina, two animal fleas that Rose Iris had met on her previous adventure.

"Oh, please can I go and speak with my friends for a while?" said Rose Iris.

"No, I'm sorry but we have to go now, for we are on a very important quest and must hurry," said Leanora. "I hope you will stop fighting now," she scolded the two hares. She could tell from the angry looks in their eyes that they would not. "Hold on tightly, Rose Iris," she said.

The two travellers headed back out of the gate and returned to the leafy lane and the pram, with the little girl clinging tightly to the hatband. The naughty hares continued their boxing match. First Giselle punched Gilliad on the nose. Then Gilliad boxed Giselle around the ears.

"Do hares always fight each other?" asked Rose Iris.

"No, not all the time, but if you visit the fields in spring you will often see them boxing," replied Leanora. "It's because the boys start thinking about love before the girls do. Of course, in this magical world everything is different, so you may see them fighting whenever they choose.

"We'll travel along the lane whilst it heads north and maybe we will find our nosey friend before we reach the stream." Leanora hoped so, for if not she would not know which way to go when they reached the end of the lane. There was a footpath that followed the bank of the stream and they would have to decide whether it would be best to follow the path to the east or the west, and she had no idea which route Nosey Nora would have taken.

Unfortunately, they didn't meet a single soul before finally arriving at the stream. Leanora wondered which way Nosey

Nora would have gone, and while she was thinking about it there was suddenly a loud flapping of wings and a horrible squawking sound. Over the tops of the trees there came flying a large, grey heron, who was making an awful fuss about where it would land. Eventually it came down into the water with a terrible splash. Both Leanora and Rose Iris were made very wet.

"Err, yuck, yuck, yuck," it complained.

"Hello, Mr. Cantlike. How are you today?" Leanora asked. She could guess what his answer would be.

"Hm! It's always the same. What am I supposed to do? I can't like it," he said.

"You can't like what?" the tiny girl called from the brim of the old Gypsy's hat.

"I can't like water; it makes me wet," he replied.

"Oh! Is that why you're wearing wellington boots?" she asked.

"Of course. You don't think I enjoy wearing these awful things, do you?" he grumbled.

"Well! if you don't like water and you don't like wellingtons, why don't you leave off the boots and land on the bank, instead of in the stream?" Rose Iris thought him extremely bad natured.

"Oh no, that would never do, yuck, yuck! I can't like mud because it makes a horrible noise when it squelches between my toes, and anyway I can't like getting them mucky," he said.

"What about the grass then?" the little girl asked. "If you land on the grass it's much drier and won't squelch through your toes."

"No, it's no good landing on grass. I can't like it when it tickles my feet."

MR CANTLIKE

"Well! As long as you don't eat me, you must do as you please, I suppose." She was beginning to lose her patience with Mr. Cantlike.

"I wouldn't eat you. I can't like anything that wears clothes," he continued to complain.

"Is there anything that you can like?" the little girl continued to call from the brim of the old felt hat.

"Yes, of course there is. I like frogs and fish for dinner." There was a long pause before he continued. "The trouble is, I can't like catching them."

"Have you seen Nosey Nora lately?" Leanora chimed in.

"Funny you should ask that question. As a matter of fact, I have just flown over her. I didn't stop to speak because . . ."

"I know! You can't like her," Rose Iris interrupted rather rudely.

"Take the path that leads to the west. She's only about half a mile away by the old railway track," he said to the old Gypsy, whilst completely ignoring the little girl's comment.

"Thank you very much for your help," Leanora said, as she began to wander over the very uneven ground with the old pots and pans jangling over the handle of the pram as usual. "Goodbye for now, Mr. Cantlike."

Rose Iris was glad she didn't have to sit on the old blanket in the pram. She was sure that the bumpy path would cause her to be thrown up into the air, out of the pram and down onto the ground.

Now, half a mile may not seem very far to travel, but Leanora never did anything very fast and so it took quite a long while before they arrived at the railway track. Unfortunately, there wasn't a sign of Nosey Nora anywhere.

"I think we must have missed her, so we should stop and have a nice cup of tea," Leanora said cheerfully, for she loved tea. So, they left the path, and she made a small wood fire in a nearby field. Rose Iris sat on a leaf and drank her tea from a tiny blade of grass that the old Gypsy had rolled into a cup shape before folding up the end to stop it from leaking.

It was whilst they were enjoying their tea that they heard a rustling sound among the tall blades of grass. Then, there was a sniffing and a scratching sound before suddenly out from between the grass stalks popped a head. The little girl could tell by the size of her snout that it was Nosey Nora. She was a bank shrew.

Rose Iris had only ever seen one shrew before, and it was very teeny tiny. That was because she herself was human sized. Now, because the little girl was so small, the shrew looked enormous. What was even more peculiar were the clothes Nosey Nora wore: a beautiful red dress, turquoise knickers, black patent shoes and a large red bow in her hair.

"Oh! How lucky we are to have found you," said Leanora. "I need to ask you something very important."

"Sorry! I can't stop, I'm on my way to my dancing lessons," Nosey Nora replied.

"I was just wondering . . ." Leanora started.

"Guess what? Gusty the wind whistler and Gritty the rock doppy drank too much rose-hip wine and they both fell into the river," continued Nosey Nora. "If it hadn't been for . . ."

"Excuse me interrupting, but I wondered if you know what has happened to Princess Mae Woo and where she is?" Leanora did not have time to gossip.

"Have you heard about Rumpy the rat?" The shrew

continued. "He sat on a piece of glass when he was searching for food on the rubbish dump, and . . ."

"You must tell me all the news next time I see you," said Leanora impatiently. "Have you heard what has happened to Princess Mae Woo?"

"I bet you didn't know about Sammy the snail," Nosey Nora continued in a very important voice. "He was enjoying a lettuce leaf when . . ."

"I'm very sorry but I really do not have time to chat," replied Leanora. "I just wondered if you know the whereabouts of the princess of China."

"Yes, of course I do," said Nosey Nora in a rather irritable voice. "Gregoran the Magician has taken her, and he is keeping her locked up in his castle. Now I'm sorry but I have already told you, I have to hurry to my dancing class. I haven't got time to stand gossiping all day. Why do you want to know anyway?" the shrew asked.

"No reason, but I'm glad you have told us, so we can head in the opposite direction. There's no way we want to go near the castle or meet Gregoran," Leanora crossed her fingers behind her back as she spoke, because she knew she was telling a very big fib.

Nosey Nora scuttled away before finally disappearing amongst the blades of grass.

"Where are we going next?" Rose Iris asked. "Aren't we going to save the princess anymore?"

"Of course, we are," said the old Gypsy.

"Then why did you tell Nosey Nora that we weren't?" the little girl was most confused.

"I warned you about telling Nosey Nora anything. If I had told her the truth, it would not be long before everyone knew

MISS NOSEY NORA

where we were going, including Gregoran. We have a very long journey ahead of us and so we do not want anything to hold us up," Leanora replied.

Very carefully the old Gypsy stamped her old, battered shoe on the fire that she had lit earlier to boil the kettle for their tea. She pulled her foot back from the hot ashes each time the heat began to warm her big toe, which protruded through a hole in the shoe. Then, when she was sure that the fire was completely out, they continued on their way towards the wizard's castle, hoping that there would not be too many dangers along the way.

In Search of Gregoran's Castle

They had only been travelling for a short while when they arrived at a forest. It was beginning to get dark and so Leanora decided that they would rest among the trees until sunrise. She collected some nuts and berries, and they ate them as they discussed their adventure so far, and what lay ahead.

"Why do I not see all of the creatures that I meet in this world when I am back in the human world?" Rose Iris asked of her friend.

"That is because we live in parallel worlds," replied the old Gypsy.

"What are parallel worlds?" said the little girl.

"Well, parallel means alongside," Leanora explained. "Both the human world and the magical world exist at the same time, but alongside each other. Only a very few humans are able to cross over from one world to the other. You and I are lucky to be able to do so."

"Why have I never seen anybody else from this world though?" Rose Iris questioned.

"Of course, you have. What about Igywanna-the-Wise and Bert the wood pigeon. You see them, don't you? Although you don't see him, Snoozlenap still sneaks in through your bedroom window when it is left open to leave you pleasant dreams. Toddy the fox lives in the fields. If you do not visit the fields when he is there, of course you won't see him," the old Gypsy replied. "Many of the creatures that live here prefer not to visit the human world because it is too dangerous."

"Why! Yes, of course, you're right. I do see Igywanna-the-wise, and poor Bert, who's toe never gets better." The little girl thought for a while. "Is it because you magic me into this world that I can cross over?"

"At this time, my dear. I do help you to cross over from one world to the other whenever I need your help, but you have a special gift, which has been given to you by the elfin folk," Leanora explained. "Remember the first time you crossed into this magical world by falling into the river? That was when the gift was bestowed on you. You and I had never even met at that time, yet you crossed over without my help. One day, you will be able to move from one world into the other whenever you wish without me assisting you, but you will have to wait a little longer, until the elfin folk are sure you are worthy of such a wonderful gift."

"Excuse me. Do you mind speaking a little more quietly? Some of us are trying to sleep," a tiny, sweet-tinkly but very sleepy voice interrupted their conversation.

Rose Iris looked up in the direction of the voice and was surprised to see sitting on a tree branch a beautiful glowing figure dressed in a long pink gown, who was as tiny as she was herself. Leanora also looked up into the tree.

"Oh! I'm dreadfully sorry, Sarazan. It was most unthoughtful of us to wake you up. I'd forgotten that there were tree nymphs in this forest," the old Gypsy apologised.

"Well, now that I am awake, Leanora, I may as well come down and meet your friend," said Sarazan. She had no wings at all, yet she was able to leave the tree branch and float

SARAZAN

softly down to sit beside Rose Iris. "Are you going anywhere interesting?" she asked.

"We are going to recue Princess Mae Woo from Gregoran the wicked wizard," Leanora replied, "but if you see Miss Nosey Nora, please do not tell her. She will tell everybody else and then Gregoran will know we are coming."

The tree nymph promised to keep their secret before asking who the little girl was.

"This is Rose Iris; she is a human child. Often, when I have to rescue somebody, she comes along with me. At this time, she is unable to travel from her world to this world without my help and the only way I can transport her is by making her tiny," replied the Gypsy.

"How nice to meet you," said the tree nymph. "I have heard about a little human called Rose Iris, but I never thought I would be lucky enough to meet you."

Leanora and Sarazan sat discussing things that were happening in the magical world for quite some time. Rose Iris spoke very little. She just sat and admired the beautiful creature.

"Well, I think I must go back to my bed now." As she spoke the nymph floated back up to the tree branch. There she settled down on a bed of turquoise silk and tucked a soft yellow pillow underneath her head. "Goodnight to you both," she said before falling instantly into a deep sleep, with her golden hair shining in the moonlight.

It was getting late, and they had to make an early start, so Leanora whispered "goodnight," as she tucked Rose Iris snugly under the old blanket in the pram.

"Goodnight," the little girl replied in a whisper, for she did not want to wake the tree nymph yet again.

Then Rose Iris heard a familiar tick-tick-ticking sound, which made her feel very tired. As she drifted into a deep sleep, Snoozlenap the dream sprinkler passed overhead on his magic carpet and sprinkled a handful of golden dust mixed with pleasant dreams over the Gypsy and the little girl and they slept soundly until morning.

As the sun rose the following day, Rose Iris awoke to the usual smell of burnt toast, a soft humming sound and the crackle of a burning fire.

Leanora was sat on a large log and was using a long piece of wood attached to a metal fork to toast the last but one slice of bread that she had left.

"Time to rise," she called across to the little girl. "We have a long way to travel today."

Rose Iris looked up to the wooden branch. The soft silk, turquoise sheets were still hanging from the branch. The pillow still lay across it, but Sarazan the tree nymph had disappeared.

The old Gypsy packed all her precious things under the blanket, put out the fire, washed her pots and pans, and dangled them over the handle of the pram. With Rose Iris sat on her hat, they set off once again on their journey.

They had not travelled far when they heard someone with a very cheerful voice singing a happy song. Leanora quickly moved Rose Iris from her hat and placed her safely underneath it.

"Hey, ho, fiddle diddle doh,
I watch which way the breezes blow.
When they whisper in my ear, I know,
That they'll tell me which way to go."

DROODLE

"Hello Droodle, you sound very happy. Where are you going on this lovely sunny morning?" asked Leanora, as a tiny rock doppy walked out from behind a bush.

"I'm always happy since Rose Iris and the flea army rescued us rock doppies from the trolls," he replied. "I am especially happy today because I am going on an adventure."

Rose Iris peeped out from under the old Gypsy's hat, where she had been hiding, then climbed up and sat on top of it amongst the berries and feathers. She remembered Droodle; he was one of the rock doppies that she met at the party after she had helped to free all the local creatures. He looked very smart in his moss-green shirt and purple pants. Across one of his shoulders he carried a long branch, attached to which was a large bright red handkerchief. It was filled with all his possessions, and it swung back and forth as he hurried along the path.

"Hello, Droodle," Rose Iris called down from the brim of the hat. "It's very good to see you again. Where are you going on your adventure?" she continued.

"Oh, I don't know right now. I shall go where the breezes take me." As he spoke, he picked a large ripe blueberry and thought he may save it for later. "Where are you going? Maybe I could keep you company," he said.

"I don't think that would be a very good thing for you to do," Leanora interrupted. "We have to save Princess Mae Woo from the wicked wizard Gregoran, but please don't tell anyone. It will be too dangerous for you."

"Oh! Please let me come," he said excitedly. "I want to do something dangerous and daring. I'll give you this lovely blueberry if you let me join you,"

"No, I'm sorry we cannot take you," the old Gypsy looked

at the beautiful blueberry and licked her lips as she spoke, but then she looked at the blueberry bush behind Droodle and saw that it was covered with many more lovely juicy berries. "We have to go now. It will take a long time to reach Gregoran's castle, and when we get there, we have to find the secret entrance into the rocks that the castle is built on." As she spoke, she picked a handful of berries and popped them into her mouth. The juices ran out over her lips and down her chin. Quickly she wiped them away with the cuff of her cardigan. "Oh bother," she said, as she realised that she had gotten blue juice all over her nice new red cardigan. If only she still had her old blue one, the stains would not have shown.

"I know where the secret entrance to the wizard's castle is," said Droodle. "If you let me come with you, I will show you where it is. Oh, by the way, you do know that it is guarded by a two-headed negradon, don't you?"

"Yes, of course I know about the negradon," Leanora fibbed. Once more she crossed her fingers tightly behind her back as she had when she fibbed to Miss Nosey Nora. "Tell me, where can we find the secret entrance to the castle?"

"I shan't tell you. Not unless you let me come along." The cheeky rock doppy pressed his lips tightly together in a very stubborn manner. He folded his arms across his chest and stamped his foot as he spoke.

"Well, in that case, I suppose we will have to let you join us, but I am warning you that this is a very dangerous journey." Leanora bent down and picked up the cheeky little fellow by the scruff of the neck as she spoke and placed him on the blanket in the old pram.

"Can I travel in the pram with Droodle?" Rose Iris asked

politely. She wondered if he may have news about Ilani and the rest of her mud fairy friends.

Leanora gently lifted the little girl down from the brim of her hat and sat her next to Droodle in the pram. Then she did something very odd. She took out from under the blanket a dingy old mirror and gazed into it for a while. It was made of rusty metal and was extremely dirty.

"Oh dear," she said. "My magic mirror is all clouded over, and I need to see how the Emperor of China's health is. There is only one thing that is strong enough to clean this mirror, and that is ogre spit. I know where to go to enter the world of the ogres, but I am too big to fit through the small entrance between the rocks. You will have to go through the tiny space, Rose Iris."

"I'll go too," said Droodle excitedly. "I'm very brave and can protect Rose Iris from the ogres."

"I suppose two of you would stand a better chance of returning safely than one. You will be able to look out for each other," said the old Gypsy. She doubted very much that Droodle was brave at all, but would give him a chance to prove that what he claimed was true. "Very well you can go too," she said.

"How will we get the ogre to spit?" asked Rose Iris.

"You don't have to. Ogres spit all the time. It's a very unpleasant habit that they have," Leanora replied.

"What will we collect the spit in?" the little girl asked.

Leanora took the tiny bottle, which she had used to hold the magic potion that had enabled her friend to become tiny again, out of her new red cardigan pocket. She unscrewed the lid to check nothing was left inside, replaced the lid, then whispered some magic words. Immediately the bottle began to shrink. It became so teeny-weeny that the little girl could fit it into her dress pocket, and so she did so. The rock doppy and the little girl continued to chat as they sat in the old pram and all three set out in search of the entrance to the ogres' kingdom. They travelled all day long and still did not arrive at their destination.

"We must stop for something to eat," said the old Gypsy after a long while. "Then I think we will have to sleep."

So Droodle shared his blueberry with Rose Iris, whilst Leanora ate some berries that she had picked from the blueberry bush, and they settled down for the night.

Into the World of Ogres

They were all up very early the following morning. Only a few blackbirds, a wren and a robin had risen before the three travellers and were singing their different songs. Unfortunately, Leanora no longer had any food under the blanket in her old pram. Her last slice of bread had become green and mouldy, and so she left Rose Iris and Droodle for a while to see if she could find something that they could eat.

It wasn't long before she returned with her arms full of twigs and a mixture of mushrooms, berries, moss and herbs. She built a small fire with the twigs and boiled the odd collection with water in one of the small saucepans that she kept hanging from the handle of the old pram. After the mixture had been cooking for a few minutes, she removed the berries, mushrooms, moss and herbs from the pot and shared the remaining liquid between two acorn cups, one each for Rose Iris and Droodle, and a small mug for herself.

The little girl and the rock doppy didn't like the smell of their breakfast. They each took a sip before screwing up their noses.

"Yuck! It's horrible," said Droodle.

"Don't be so fussy," said the old Gypsy. "You must drink it up because it's good for you. It may not taste very nice, but it might be the last meal you will have today."

Rose Iris said nothing. She closed her eyes, took a deep breath, then a large mouthful of the liquid and swallowed it as fast as she could. She thought of her favourite cereal, how delicious it was and how nasty this tasted, but she didn't want to hurt Leanora's feelings by complaining. After all, the old Gypsy would not have given them such an awful meal if she could have found something tastier for them.

Droodle took a few small sips before pulling a face and emptying the remaining liquid onto the ground. "Not drinking that horrible stuff. It makes me feel sick," he said.

"As you please, but you may wish you hadn't been so fussy when you feel hungry later today," said Leanora.

As they continued their journey Droodle fell fast asleep and Rose Iris returned to travel on the old felt hat. It wasn't very long before the old Gypsy stopped by a clump of large rocks, at the bottom of which was an opening. She gave the rock doppy a poke with her weatherworn finger to wake him up. He hated being woken from his sleep. So, rather blurry eyed and very grumpy, he complained bitterly.

"You will have to go through the opening in this rock alone. I can't tell you what the world is like on the other side because I have never been there. There is a spell that keeps anyone larger than an ogre from using magic to go there, and I'm much too big to go through the opening," said Leanora.

She hated letting them go without her into a world she had never seen and knew nothing about, but there was no other way to get the ogre spit. She asked Rose Iris to check that the teeny-weeny bottle was still in her pocket, before lifting her down from her hat and setting her on the ground just outside the entrance to what looked like a tiny cave. Droodle had by this time woken up properly and insisted on going into the world of ogres too.

"I will wait impatiently for you to return," Leanora said as the two small people entered the opening.

At first there was plenty of room to pass through, but as they travelled farther inside the cave, the rocks became closer and closer together, and the space between them became tighter and tighter until there was only a crack to pass through. They found it hard to squeeze between the rocks and Rose Iris thought she might get stuck and have to stay forever trapped inside the cave. They breathed in as much as they could and stretched themselves as tall as possible so they would become thinner, then they squeezed and squeezed until at last they came out on the other side of the opening.

"We are safely on the other side," the little girl's voice echoed as she called back to Leanora.

"Don't forget to be very careful and mind you don't lose the bottle," Leanora called back.

This world was not at all what Rose Iris expected it to be. She looked about in amazement. First, she said "ooh," and then she said "aah." When she had read books about ogres they had always lived in dark, dingy caves. This was a most beautiful place. There were trees covered in blossom, bamboo plants, bushes covered in berries and lots of other trees covered in fruit. The sun shone brightly, and lovely scents filled the air.

They did not know where to start looking for an ogre, but since there was only one grassy pathway, they decided to walk along it until they came to a place where they would have to decide which way to go. It wasn't very long before they reached a crossroads. In the middle of the path there was a large signpost. On one side of the signpost was an arrow that pointed, "To the Castle", and on the other side the arrow pointed "To the Woods."

Whilst they were deciding the best route to take, there came a very loud thump, thump, thumping sound. They realised that it was footsteps and quickly hid behind some rocks that were sheltered by bamboo grass, where they would be hidden from view. The footsteps became louder and louder. Then to their amazement, out from among the trees that lined the path stomped a large and very green THING.

"He can't be an ogre," whispered Rose Iris. For he did not look even a little bit scary. As a matter of fact, he had a very kind and friendly face.

Suddenly the rock doppy's tummy began to rumble very loudly. The THING stopped walking, put his hand up to cup his ear and turned his head to listen and look about him.

"Shush," whispered Rose Iris, "he will find us."

"I can't help it. I'm so hungry. It's that awful breakfast rolling about inside me," Droodle replied. Then his tummy rumbled once more. This time it was even louder.

"I know I heard a peculiar noise," said the THING. "Is somebody there?"

"Are we going to go out into the open and speak to him?" whispered Rose Iris.

"Well, you may be, but I'm not going out there. He's much too big and ugly, and he's got sticky up hair," the rock doppy whispered back.

The little girl took one look at Droodle's hair but made no comment. "Very well," she said and slowly but very carefully she crept out into the open.

"Oh! Hi little thing, why are you hiding behind that rock?" he said, so loudly that Rose Iris almost ran back into her hiding place.

"Well sir, I am a little afraid of you. You may be an ogre

and I have heard awful stories about ogres. You aren't going to eat me, are you?" she asked.

"Don't be silly, I wouldn't eat such a tiny thing. You would get stuck in my lovely teeth. Of course, I'm an ogre. What are you anyway?"

"I'm a little girl," she replied.

"Oh no! not a human being I hope?" he shouted. "We have put a spell around our world to keep humans out. Everywhere they go they destroy their world. Now they are thinking of going up to the moon and Mars, and I expect they will destroy those places next. We do not want them to ruin our world also." He paused and drew in a deep breath, before making a gurgling noise in his throat. Then he turned his head to the right and spat out an enormous dollop of grungy, green spit. "Pardon me," he said in a polite and much softer voice, for he could see that the little girl was still afraid of him.

"If you don't eat little things like me, what do you eat?" Rose Iris asked. She was beginning to feel less afraid of him. "Do you eat slugs and snails? That's what all my books say ogres eat."

"Don't be disgusting. If I ate a slug, I am sure it would make me sick, and snails would be very crunchy and would stick in my throat. No, we ogres like fruit, especially nice green apples. That's how I keep my skin so beautiful," he replied as he drew in another deep breath. Once more he made a loud gurgling noise in his throat before turning his head to the left, because he didn't want to spit on the little girl. Out from his mouth came another enormous glob of nasty slimy spit. It shot through the air, over the rock, through the bamboo grass and landed on top of poor Droodle.

PRINCE IGOR

"Ugh, that slimy stuff landed on top of me," said the rock doppy as he crept out from his hiding place. "Why don't you look where you're spitting?"

"Oh! I see we have another visitor," said the ogre. "Now that I can see you, I will avoid spitting in your direction. Can I offer you something to eat, or a lovely drop of rose-hip wine? I believe rock doppies love a drop of rose-hip wine."

"No thank you, sir, but I would like to know your name? I'm Rose Iris and this brave fellow is Droodle," the little girl replied.

"I'm Prince Igor. My father is King Delgora; he is the ruler of this beautiful world," replied the ogre.

"Why did you say no thank you without asking me first? I am starving," whispered Droodle, as he struggled to move since he was covered in ogre spit.

"We have not got time to waste eating and drinking. Leanora will be waiting impatiently for the ogre spit. We have to go right now, and you should say you are hungry and not that you are starving, because you aren't," Rose Iris replied.

"Don't be daft, we haven't collected the spit yet," said the rock doppy in a rather impudent manner.

"I hope you don't think us rude," said Rose Iris. "It has been very nice meeting you, Your Highness, but if you will excuse us, we will have to go now. You see we are on a very important quest and there is no time to lose," she continued. She wished she could spend longer and become good friends with this dear, gentle person, but it was not possible. She decided that when she returned to the human world, she would tell everyone that ogres may not necessarily be as evil as writers said they were, neither might they all live in dark dingy caves.

The rock doppy was puzzled and very annoyed. Not only had they missed a chance to enjoy a good meal, but they were returning to Leanora without the one thing they had come to collect, but he kept his thoughts to himself.

They all said their goodbyes and the two tiny people made their way back to the opening in the rocks, which allowed them to enter this beautiful world, with Droodle complaining continually. Once again Rose Iris squeezed with difficulty through the crack, but Droodle had slipped through ahead of her quite easily.

"See! I have become so skinny that I can easily pass through the opening," Droodle complained.

Rose Iris knew that it was not because he had become skinny, but she herself was stuck tightly and beginning to be afraid. Once more the little girl breathed herself in, but this time she was unable to escape from the grip of the rock.

"Oh! Flibberty jibberty, I wish you would open," she said in a very frightened voice, for she knew Leanora could not come and rescue her. She continued to push and push but was stuck too tightly in the crack. Then, all of a sudden, there was a creaking sound, followed by a cracking noise that echoed all around her. To the little girl's amazement, the crack in the rock slowly began to widen and she could walk through the gap with plenty of room to spare. When she at last stepped out from the opening and back into the fresh air, her friends were waiting for her.

"Thank you for working your magic, Leanora," she said.

"What magic?" replied the old Gypsy.

"She's forgotten to collect the ogre spit," said the rock

doppy in a snooty, sing-song manner. "You should have put me in charge; I wouldn't have forgotten."

"No, she hasn't," said Leanora as she picked him up by his ankles, then, after tipping him upside down, used the gooey ogre spit that was still matted in his hair to wipe her magic mirror. Immediately the mirror began to clear. It got brighter and brighter, until at last it glistened in the sunshine.

Next Leanora filled one of her old pots with water and dropped the rock doppy headfirst into it. Then she collected a handful of grass and used it to scrub him clean. He certainly looked much cleaner and smelt much pleasanter when she finally took him out from the pot and dried him roughly with a piece of old rag. Unfortunately, he also looked much redder because it had taken a great deal of scrubbing to get him clean. It wasn't only the scrubbing which made him so red. Droodle hated washing and had fought and struggled all the time he was in the pot, so he was in a very bad temper indeed.

The old Gypsy held the magic mirror close to her face so she could look deeply into it and whispered some magic words, which the little girl could not hear very well. From where she sat on the old lady's felt hat, she could see a swirl of mist form inside the mirror. As it began to clear, she noticed that the glass reflected a very sad picture. The Emperor of China lay on an ornately carved wooden bed. He was covered in the most beautiful, embroidered bedclothes made of gold silk. His wife, the empress, sat by his side wiping the tears from his swollen, red eyes.

"Oh no!" said Leanora. "The emperor is getting sicker and sicker. We really will have to hurry, or we will be too late to save him before he falls into a deep sleep from which he will never wake up." Then she wriggled her nose before taking a deep sniff.

Rose Iris and Droodle also wriggled their noses.

"Phew! Leanora. What's that horrible smell?" said the little girl. "It smells like pooh."

"That's not pooh. It's a stinky-yabberwak." The old Gypsy recognised the awful stench immediately.

"What's a stinky-yabberwak?" Rose Iris had never heard of such a thing.

"It's the wizard's familiar. Now the yabberwak has seen us he will report back to Gregoran."

"What is a familiar?" asked the little girl.

"A familiar is the magical world's word for what humans call a pet," said Leanora. "A stinky-yabberwak is a flying creature that the wizard uses to spy on people. Lucky for us it smells so nasty that it cannot hide for long without us knowing it is nearby. If it saw us looking in the mirror and also noticed that we were watching the emperor, it will tell Gregoran. The magician will know why we are coming and will try to stop us freeing Princess Mae Woo. So, we must find the yabberwak and keep it prisoner."

Leanora began to hunt under the bushes and behind rocks, stones and tree trunks. Suddenly something ran from behind a clump of grass. It was green, had a long tail and very large wings for such a small creature. "There he is," she shouted, before taking off her lovely felt hat and throwing it over the horrible little thing. The hat wriggled and began to run about all over the place because the yabberwak was trying to escape from beneath it, but Leanora grabbed it and held on tightly with both hands. Still, it continued to wriggle. The yabberwak started to screech and shouted awful sounding words in his own language. Rose Iris was sure they must be naughty swear words.

The old Gypsy carefully lifted up a small section of her hat with one hand and held the other hand ready to catch the little blighter, but it gave her the slip and ran as fast as it could before taking a running leap, spreading its wings and flying up onto a tree branch. He stood there amongst the branches for only a few seconds before opening his wings once more and flying off into the distance.

Leanora picked up her hat and put it back on her head. "Oh dear, I think the stinky-yabberwak is still nearby," she complained. "It still stinks around here." As she spoke, she lifted Rose Iris from the ground and placed her back on top of the hat.

"Phew! It's not the yabberwak. It's your stinky hat. If you don't mind, I'll travel in your cardigan pocket for a while until the smell disappears," said the little girl.

Leanora lifted Rose Iris down from her hat and placed her gently into her pocket. Then she took off the hat and placed it on the tray beneath the old pram. That was when she noticed that her water supply had gotten very low.

"We must hurry to the castle, but first I will have to go down to a stream that is nearby and fill my container with water, or we will have nothing to drink as well as nothing to eat," she said.

THE STINKY YABBERWAK

The Vain Mrs Otterby

They soon arrived at the stream. The old Gypsy removed the plastic container that she kept under the old pram and hurried down to where the water lapped against the bank. Rose Iris stood in Leanora's cardigan pocket and Droodle remained in the pram, where he had fallen fast asleep after his ordeal with the ogre, followed by the shock of having his lovely red hair used as a scrubbing brush to clean the magic mirror.

Suddenly, there was a loud splash and something that was extremely large sprang out of the stream. It was an otter dressed in a blue and yellow striped swimsuit.

"Does my bum look big in this, Leanora?" she said. "Don't worry about hurting my feelings. I want an honest answer."

Leanora looked at the otter as it swirled around and waddled up and down like a duck. She didn't want to hurt her feelings, but she didn't want to tell any more lies either.

"Well, it is rather tight dear, especially around the bottom. I know it is not that your bottom is too big, Mrs. Otterby, but that the swimming suit is a little small," said the old Gypsy. "You have such lovely thick fur that it is making the swim-suit swell out around your hips."

"Hmm," said the otter. "Are you sure you are telling the truth? Come now, you mustn't be jealous. I know it is hard to compete with someone as beautiful as I am, but I really do need an honest opinion."

"I certainly like your new swimsuit," said Leanora. So far

MRS OTTERBY

that was not a lie. "I liked your old one better though." Still not a lie.

"You still haven't answered my question," said Mrs. Otterby. "Why is it so hard to admit that I look gorgeous?"

"Why have you got a new swimsuit anyway?" asked the old Gypsy. "Your old, slightly larger suit was perfect for you and most becoming for your figure."

"I know, but it was starting to stretch and become baggy around the middle," said the otter. "Now give me an honest answer. Does my bum look big in this?"

Leanora was beginning to get angry. She didn't have time to waste speaking to this vain creature when she should be hurrying to the wizard's castle to rescue Princess Mae Woo, before her father died of a broken heart. Either she would have to tell another lie or tell the truth and upset the otter.

"Yes, your bottom does look big in your new swimsuit," she blurted out at last.

Mrs. Otterby's face began to turn red. Then it became redder, before turning a dark purple. "How could you be so rude and unkind? I can't believe you would find it so hard to tell the truth. I'll never ask your opinion again. In future I'll ask someone who will tell the truth." She turned her back on Leanora and dived back into the water. Then she swam away until she disappeared, leaving a stream of frothy bubbles behind her.

"You mean you'll keep asking people until you find someone who will lie to you," said the old Gypsy as she took the lid off the plastic container and dipped it in the water to refill it. "Now, we must be on our way," she said as she climbed back up the bank of the stream, returned to the old pram and carefully placed the water container back underneath it.

Rose Iris, who had been watching and listening from the safety of Leanora's pocket, had said nothing at all whilst her friend and Mrs. Otterby were discussing the swimsuit, but she decided that she did not like the otter very much at all.

Arriving at Gregoran's Castle

They had only travelled a short way when they spotted far in the distance the dark grey castle perched high on top of an ugly, rocky mountain. It was obvious from the way the purple flags that hung from two of the turrets flapped and wriggled that it was very windy around the castle. A weathervane also spun one way then the other as the wind swirled around it.

"How are we going to get to the top of the rocky mountain? Do you know a magic spell?" Rose Iris asked the old Gypsy.

"Even I cannot work a spell that could take us to the top of a mountain. No, we will have to find the secret entrance," said Leanora.

"I told you I know where it is," Droodle felt very important. "Let me sit on your hat so I can see where we are going, and I will show you how to find it."

So, they set off in the direction of the castle. Both Rose Iris and Droodle sat on the old Gypsy's hat. Leanora had to walk for a very long time before they arrived at the bottom of the rocky mountain upon which the castle stood.

Droodle guided them around the rocks until they arrived at a place where they noticed a secret door that was set in a grey stone wall. The door would be large enough for Leanora to walk through. It was well hidden by plants, which grew up and over it. They did not approach it straight away but hid

GREGORAN'S CASTLE

behind a nearby tree, since there was, curled around the branch of another tree above the door, what looked like a giant snake. It had two heads and each head had two horns.

"Oh dear, even I can't like negradons," Leanora shuddered as she spoke. "They are so slimy and sly."

"I want to go and travel west," suddenly one the heads complained, as it stretched and pulled in a westerly direction. "Then I can slither in amongst the potatoes that are being sent to America. I've always wanted to go there but you won't let me go," he moaned.

"Why should I," said the other head, "when I want to go east to Africa, India and Japan but you won't come with me?" The other head stretched and tugged in the opposite direction to the first.

This gave Leanora a great idea. She placed Rose Iris and Droodle safely in the pram before walking out into the open, where she could be seen by the negradon, but not close enough for it to grab her and squeeze her until all her breath was gone.

"Do you not realise, that is why Gregoran has placed you in that tree?" she said. "He knows that because one half of you wants to travel west, whilst the other half wants to go east, you will never be able to move from this spot because you are both pulling in different directions."

"Who are you?" hissed both heads at once. "Won't you come a little closer so we can see you properly?" they continued hissing.

Leanora moved a little closer, but not close enough for the negradon to grab her, squeeze out her life and gobble her up.

"Well, what do you suggest is the best way to move from this spot if we cannot agree in which direction we should go?" said one of the heads.

THE NEGRADON

"In which direction we should go?" repeated the other head.

"You have three choices. Either I make you disappear, or I use one of my magic spells to turn you into two different creatures," said Leanora. There was no way she was going any closer to the horrible negradon.

"That is only two choices," said one head.

"Only two choices," repeated the second head.

"Please allow me to finish speaking before rudely interrupting," said the old Gypsy. "The third choice is to remain as you are, joined together and never to move from that branch."

Both heads stopped pulling and tugging. They turned to face each other. They whispered quietly together so the old Gypsy would not hear what they were saying.

"That is a very good idea," said one.

"Very good idea," said the other.

"You must use your magic to help us to go in different directions," said the first. "We do not like either of the other choices."

"Either of the other choices," said the second.

Leanora returned to the old pram where Rose Iris and Droodle were hiding patiently. She felt for something under the old blanket until finally she pulled out a red book. On the cover it had the word "SPELLS". After opening it up, she flipped over the pages, every now and again stopping to read something until she found what she was looking for. Then she returned to the negradon.

"Are you sure this is what you want to happen to you?" she asked. "You must promise to go your own ways and leave me alone, if I help you to escape from that branch," she continued.

"Yes of course. It is a wonderful idea, and we promise you will be left alone," both heads replied at the same time, for they had become very excited.

Leanora took her magic wand out from where it was hidden up her cardigan sleeve. She held the spell book in one hand and the wand in the other. Sometimes she turned the pages forward and sometimes she flipped them backwards until once more she found the spell she was looking for. "Aah!" she said as she raised the wand and pointed it in the direction of the negradon, speaking these magic words as she did so.

"Itsma, bitsma capstimandoo,
When one cannot agree, it must become two."

First Leanora waved her wand in a circular movement. Then she moved it from left to right, before waving it up and down and pointing it once again in the direction of the negradon. Two blue lights left the end of the wand and whizzed toward the creature, hitting each of its heads right on its nose.

All four eyes of the negradon grew larger. They became circled with purple and pink. Then suddenly the creature began to split down the middle and turned into two different animals. It was no longer one negradon but had become two. Now they looked even more like snakes.

"Thank you," said the creature who wanted to travel west.

"I am very grateful," said the other. "Now I can go east and visit all the countries I have always wanted to see."

All this time Rose Iris and Droodle were unable to see what was happening because they had been hiding safely in the pram behind the tree, but they were able to hear the conversation.

Leanora now brought the pram into the open and she and her tiny friends watched as the two halves of the negradon slithered off in different directions and disappeared into the bushes.

Through the Secret Door

It was time to enter the secret door, but Leanora did not want Droodle to accompany them. She felt that his presence may put herself and Rose Iris in danger, since it would be one extra person to make mistakes. So, she had to think of a good excuse to leave him behind, without making him feel that they did not want his company and hurting his feelings. That was when she had a really great idea.

"Oh dear, dear me, Droodle. What am I to do? I need somebody brave and strong to guard my precious pram and all the special things that I have under the blanket. I wonder who it should be," as she spoke, she winked secretly to Rose Iris.

"I will stay behind if you like," said the little girl.

"Oh no, no, you would not be brave enough, or wise enough. This is a very important thing to have to do." Once again, the old Gypsy gave Rose Iris a crafty wink.

"No, let me do it," said Droodle full of his own importance. "I am very brave, and you will not have to worry that I will fall asleep and fail to keep watch."

"No, I do not think you could do such an important job," Leanora replied.

"I will, I promise," the rock doppy stamped his foot on the blanket as he spoke.

This was another reason Leanora did not want Droodle to accompany them. He was inclined to be rather naughty if he did not always get his own way. As a matter of fact, he could be a pain in the bottom.

"Very well I will trust you to stay and guard everything." The old Gypsy's plan to leave Droodle behind had worked.

She made sure her wand was safely tucked up her sleeve, for she was sure that it would be needed when they entered the castle. She picked up Rose Iris from the pram and placed her carefully on the felt hat. It had ceased to smell disgusting by this time, although it still didn't smell particularly pleasant either. Then they set off towards the secret door, waving to Droodle as they went.

The old Gypsy turned the doorknob and to her amazement the door creaked open. Once inside they found themselves in a long, dark passageway. The only light came from torches, which decorated the walls. These were placed so far apart that although there was ample light as they passed by one torch, it was nearly pitch black halfway before they reached the next. Rose Iris clung tightly to Leanora's hat. If she fell off halfway between the torches, the old Gypsy may never be able to find her in the dark.

After a while they reached a large open area from which a wide stairway stretched and curved up into the darkness. Tiny glows of light flickered and twinkled above them, so they knew the torches continued to light the staircase, even though the stairs themselves disappeared into the darkness above. Along one side of the stairs there was a rope fixed to the wall.

"This is the way we must go," said Leanora. "Thank goodness for the rope. It is so dark up there we will hardly be able to see where we are going." So, she grabbed the rope tightly with her left hand and slowly began to climb the staircase.

The old Gypsy huffed and puffed as she began to lose her breath. Every now and then she would stop and sit on a step to rest her legs. She would take a few deep breaths before standing up and once more continuing her climb. The stairs were very steep and seemed to go on forever. Rose Iris continued to hang on tightly to the hatband until at last they reached a landing. The little girl had been counting the steps as they climbed them. There were exactly one hundred. Leanora closed her eyes and lowered her head, since she was completely exhausted. When she stopped huffing and puffing and her breathing returned to normal, she lifted her head, then gave a gasp.

"Oh, no," she said in a very tired voice. "Not more stairs."

So, they began to climb another staircase and were relieved when there were only about twenty more steps before reaching what appeared to be a large cave. Leanora's heavy breathing echoed around the place, and as they whispered softly to each other even their whispers sounded as if there were hundreds of voices present, for they echoed and overlapped each other long after the two frightened people had stopped whispering.

They walked through the cave until at last they reached a bridge that crossed an enormous, dark, black empty space. There was a big problem, because the bridge ended halfway across the gaping hole in the ground.

"What are we going to do now?" asked Rose Iris as she peeped over the top of Leanora's hat and saw the broken bridge and the deep hole. Beneath it was a vast space that seemed to go on and on forever. At the bottom of the hole red hot flames soared up towards them and a red, boiling river swirled beneath the flames. The air was filled with a nasty smoky smell and they became hotter and hotter and redder and redder.

Neither of them spoke for a while, whilst the old Gypsy considered how she could find a way to cross the gaping hole. Suddenly she reached down towards the ground. Picking up a handful of dust she threw it over the piece of bridge that was missing. Both Leanora and Rose Iris were amazed to see that instead of floating down into the empty space below, the dust settled on what appeared to be an invisible walkway. This proved that the bridge was still there, although Gregoran the magician must have made it invisible. The sides had broken away and it had become very narrow, but at least they would be able to continue their journey.

"I am going to put you into my cardigan pocket," said Leanora. "You will be much safer there." As she spoke, she removed the little girl from the top of her hat and tucked her safely into her pocket. If the old Gypsy lost her footing, she would tumble down into the hole and into the boiling hot river, taking Rose Iris with her, but at least now her little friend could not fall from her hat and disappear alone into the swirling hot liquid below.

Leanora carefully put one foot in front of the other, hoping that she would not lose her balance, miss her step and go tumbling into the dark space below them. She held her arms out straight to each side like a tightrope walker, but every so often she would begin to wobble and have to stop and steady herself until, at last, they reached the other side of the hole. She sighed loudly as both her feet stood firmly on solid ground. All this time Rose Iris had sat silently in the old Gypsy's pocket, but hearing Leanora's sigh of relief made her feel brave and once more she peeped her head over the top of the pocket.

"Look, there is a trap door and a wooden ladder reaching

up to it," she said. "Do you think we will be able to go through there?"

"Of course. We will have to try, but I'm not sure what will be waiting on the other side," said her friend. "Do you want to stay in my pocket, or would you rather return to my hat?"

"On your hat please," said the tiny girl.

So, the old Gypsy reached down into her pocket and lifted Rose Iris out gently before placing her carefully on her old felt hat.

Then she walked over to the ladder and climbed it. The trap door was tightly closed and had a thick iron chain hanging from it. The ends of the chain were held securely together by a large, heavy lock. Leanora pulled as hard as she could to try to pull the lock apart, but it would not open.

Slowly but carefully, she climbed back down the ladder and began to hunt upon the ground to find something that she could use to break the lock. Unfortunately, there was nothing. Not a rock, nor a piece of wood, or anything else that would help them. Then she had a very clever idea. She climbed back up the ladder and took her magic wand out from where it was tucked safely inside her cardigan sleeve. Then she pushed the tip of the wand into the opening between the lock and the hook that kept it closed tightly. She whispered some magic words and after a few pushes and pulls the lock burst open. She did not notice that the end of her beautiful wand had also broken off. She didn't hear the soft, gentle tap as it hit the ground below, then rolled and tumbled secretly down into a dark crevice, never to be seen again.

Leanora slowly and carefully pushed the trap door up and lowered it quietly onto the stone floor above. Then she popped her head up through the opening. Only the top of her old felt hat, upon which sat Rose Iris, and the old Gypsy's eyes protruded from the opening in the floor. The trap door had opened to reveal that they were at last about to enter the castle. They had arrived in the middle of a long passageway. Everything was grey. Grey stone walls led along grey stone floors. Leanora crawled with difficulty out from the opening and into the passage.

She dusted herself down then began to creep quietly along the passage. Every so often they passed under a grey archway. As in the tunnel the walls were lit by torches that flickered and threw shadows on the opposite walls. There was a nasty smell, which warned them that a stinky-yabberwak had recently passed along that way before them.

Then they heard voices. There were at least two people speaking and the voices came from a room ahead, into which the door was almost closed. Only a small crack allowed the voices, one deep and gruff, and the other high pitched, almost screeching, to be heard from the passageway. Leanora noticed a keyhole and bent down to look through the opening, hoping to see who the voices belonged to. She was surprised to see that on the other side, beside a large, round, wooden table, and looking at some kind of plan, stood Gregoran the magician and Petrina the witch. Also, on the table there lay sleeping soundly the stinky-yabberwak.

As usual Petrina was dressed in her favourite long black frock, pulled in at the waist with a black cord decorated with black tassels. On her head she wore her high-pointed, black hat with a very wide brim.

Gregoran wore more colourful clothes, a beautiful green cloak and a long purple robe that reached down almost to the floor. Only his brown pointed shoes could be seen protruding beneath the robe. On his head he wore a very similar hat to Petrina's, and his left hand was clenched around a long wooden tree branch that reached right down to the ground.

"You must go and find a hiding place. Be very careful and very silent," as she whispered, Leanora lifted the little girl down from her hat and placed her gently on the cold stone floor by the tiny crack between the door and its frame.

Rose Iris said nothing in reply. She took a few steps into the opening and popped her head slowly around the door. When she saw the wizard and the witch with their heads so closely together that their hats were almost touching, and discussing their plans, she was horrified.

"We can't go in there," she whispered as she retraced her steps. "Not only is there a wizard but also Petrina the witch is in there."

"I know. No need to worry, my magic is very strong, and I will be able to use it on both of them. Petrina is no problem, though Gregoran may prove to be a little more difficult," her friend replied.

So, once more the tiny little girl crept through the opening between the door and its frame. This time, she tiptoed softly and silently across the room and found a safe hiding place behind the leg of a chair. She held her hand over her nose and tried not to breath because the awful smell of the yabberwak filled the air and made her feel sick. Of course, it was impossible not to breath and at last she had to take a deep breath, which made the stinky smell even stronger. Neither the witch nor the wizard caught sight of her.

Once Leanora saw through the keyhole that Rose Iris was safely hidden, she flung open the door and entered the room.

"What are you two evil creatures up to now?" she shouted. "Why have you taken Princess Mae Woo from her dear parents, Gregoran?"

"So, you have come at last," replied the wizard. "We have been waiting for you ever since my little familiar here reported seeing you looking in your magic mirror and speaking about the princess's father." As he spoke, he fondly stroked the yabberwak, who stirred but did not wake up.

"You, you will not be able to make me disappear from this story like you did the previous one," screamed Petrina in a screeching, ear-piercing voice.

"Oh, be quiet Petrina," said Leanora. "I am sick of your stupid chatter." As she spoke, she took her wand from her sleeve and pointed it at the evil witch. "Destardo excabardo zorabora rat," she said. The wand spluttered and a tiny blue light puffed out of it, but instead of shooting towards Petrina it fell onto the floor and burst into a cloud of blue dust before disappearing completely.

Petrina just cackled with laughter and waited to see what would happen next. This was a very bad mistake to make.

Leanora couldn't understand. She had never had trouble with her magic before. What a surprise she got when she saw what had happened to her beautiful wand. When she had used it to open the trapdoor, she had chipped off the end and now it did not work as well as it should. She gave it a shake before trying again.

"Destardo excabardo zorabora rat," she cried.

This time the blue light shot from the end of the wand and with great force hit Petrina on the nose. She began to shiver and shake, before jumping up and down. Then her toes left the floor and she ended up spinning around and around on her heels. Gradually she became smaller and smaller. As she shrank, she started to grow hair all over her face. Then her gigantic nose became pointed and whiskers grew from it. Hairy ears that were pink on the inside formed on the top of her head. She continued spinning around and around before finally disappearing under her dreadful black clothes and hat.

The other three people in the room stared at the pile of clothes and noticed that there was movement underneath them. Then a pink nose popped out, followed by a hairy face with tiny, black, frightened, beady eyes. Gradually from beneath the pile of black material there emerged a creature. Rose Iris realised it was a gigantic rat with a very long

PETRINA

skinny tail. It crept out looking very afraid. Then with a lot of screeching and jabbering in a language nobody could understand, it scuttled towards the open door and out of the room. Of course, the rat was not as large as it seemed to the little girl, but this was the first time she had seen a rat whilst she was so tiny.

"You will not stop me from having a beautiful menagerie, Leanora," shouted the wizard in a loud voice that echoed all around the room. "I want to form a zoo with all the most beautiful animals, and if I find that certain animals no longer exist, I will make them by magic. I had a spell that would make a most wonderful creature, but I needed a Chinese princess to make the magic work," as he spoke, he lifted his long wooden stick and pointed it towards Leanora. "Destardo excabardo zorabora beaver," he shouted.

"Ditsigo waggertag, stop this spell," the old Gypsy lifted her wand as she spoke and pointed it towards the wizard. A small blue twinkle appeared at the end of her wand. It spluttered and splattered before finally dropping to the ground and fading away.

Rose Iris put her hands over her eyes and closed them tightly as she remained hidden behind the chair leg. She could not bear to see what was about to happen to Leanora. There was a cracking sound followed by a whirring sound and a whizzing noise, then a loud pop, before everything gradually became silent.

After a while, the little girl opened her eyes very slowly and was amazed to see Leanora had gone. She knew the old Gypsy would not leave her in such a dangerous place. "Gregoran must have worked a spell to make my dear friend disappear," she thought. Then she noticed on the floor lay two piles of clothes. One belonged to Petrina, and she was horrified to see that the second pile was made up of a brown skirt, a red cardigan and a beautiful felt hat that was decorated with flowers, berries and feathers. One old brown shoe with a hole in the toe protruded from under the skirt, and a golden locket lay beside it. Leanora had completely vanished. The yabberwak had woken up, and cowering in a corner stood a large animal. It was much bigger than Petrina the rat, but shorter than Toddy the fox, although it was very much plumper and had long thick fur.

Gregoran used one of his brown shoes to move the animal from the corner. Then he tucked the toe of the shoe under the poor creature's bottom and gave it a rough push into a nearby cage and locked the door tightly shut. Then he followed his precious yabberwak out of the room, looking very pleased with himself. "Stupid witch," he said as he disappeared into the passage outside.

"Leanora, where are you?" Rose Iris whispered. She was afraid she would not get a reply, for she could not see her friend anywhere in the room.

"Here I am. Just wait till I get a new wand. Then that stupid wizard will be sorry. He will regret calling me a stupid witch."

"I can't see you. Where are you hiding?" said the little girl

"Why here of course. In the cage. That stupid wizard has turned me into a beaver."

"I don't like to be cheeky, Leanora, but maybe it was you who was a little stupid to challenge both Gregoran and Petrina at the same time." Rose Iris passed easily between the bars of the cage as she spoke.

"Well, I didn't know the end of my wand had broken off,

GREGORAN

and my spells would not work properly, did I? Huh, that stupid wizard has put me into this stupid cage. What a stupid thing to do," the old Gypsy continued to grumble. "I'm not stupid. What do you think this cage is made from?" she asked.

"Why, wood of course," said the little girl.

"Yes, and what am I at this embarrassing moment?" as she spoke Leanora raised her front lip and showed her long, sharp front teeth.

"Oh, of course, you're a beaver, and beaver's love to eat and chew wood all the time. Gregoran is certainly very, very stupid." Rose Iris clapped her hands excitedly as she spoke. "Do you have a plan? Surely you won't have to stay a beaver forever."

"First, we will have to find the boobar tree. There is one not far from the entrance to Gregoran's castle, but we will need to go back through the trapdoor, return down the staircase and through the door that was guarded by the negradon. I will have to make a new wand. The trouble is, it will not work strong spells until it has been enchanted by the elfin Queen Vilabria. So, when it has been shaped to the perfect proportions, we will have to find her. The elves live only a short distance from the boobar tree, so they should be easy to find."

In Search of the Boobar Tree

So, Leanora nibbled her way through the bars of the cage. Using her teeth, she took hold of her brown skirt, red cardigan and brown socks from the pile of clothes that lay scattered on the floor in the centre of the room. Sadly, she was unable to carry all her clothes, so left behind her many jumpers, shoes and beautiful felt hat. She crouched down to allow Rose Iris to climb up her thick strands of fur and onto her back. Then, with the few clothes she had managed to gather, she started her journey back towards the door that had allowed them to enter the castle.

"Hang on tightly," Leanora whispered as she skuttled out of the room, along the passageway and through the trap door, before climbing with difficulty down the wooden ladder. Rose Iris clung tightly to the old Gypsy's fur, for she was running extremely fast. The beaver continued down one set of stairs and across the broken bridge before finally running down the one hundred steps and along another passageway towards the secret door, which had given them entry to Gregoran's castle. It seemed to take no time at all, for Leanora the beaver moved faster than Leanora the Gypsy.

At last, they arrived back at the old pram. Droodle was nowhere to be seen and Leanora the beaver was unable to climb up into the pram. He was probably fast asleep and not guarding the pram at all, which was a very good thing, since the old Gypsy worried that if he awoke, he might insist on accompanying them and maybe he would endanger their journey by being naughty.

Quietly they crept away in the direction of the boobar tree and it wasn't long before they found what Leanora was looking for. On a bank running alongside a stream, it stood alone on a mound of mud. It was not a very big tree, and nothing about it suggested that it was special or magical. As a matter of fact, it looked very ordinary to Rose Iris.

Leanora the beaver placed the clothes she had been carrying on the bank of the stream, before allowing Rose Iris to climb down her fur to stand beside them. Then she scrambled onto a pile of logs and began selecting a small branch the perfect size and shape to make her new wand. When she had decided which branch would be ideal, she nibbled at it until it was ready to fall from the tree.

"Look out, Rose Iris. Stand well away," she shouted. Suddenly the branch made a creaking noise before slowly breaking from the tree and falling with a dull thud onto the muddy bank.

This made the poor tree look even smaller, but all of a sudden, a puff of silver dust appeared in the exact place on the trunk of the tree that the branch had been gnawed from. Then, to the little girl's surprise, a brand-new branch began growing. It grew until it was exactly the same size and a perfect copy of the original branch. That was when Rose Iris realised that this really was a magical tree.

Leanora the beaver chewed and nibbled at the branch before raising it up towards the sky in her clenched paw. "Tut, tut, oh no," she said, "that's not exactly how I want you to look." Then she chewed and nibbled some more.

GUESS WHO?

"That's better, now you are perfect," she mumbled as she held it up to the sky once more. Then to Rose Iris's amazement the beaver chewed her beautiful new wand in half. Well! not quite in half, because one piece was a little smaller than the other. Next, she placed the smaller piece of the branch on the ground and waved the larger piece in the air. "Destardo, excabardo, zorabora witch," she uttered.

Rose Iris was amazed to see a shining blue light appear from the end of the new wand; it did a little dance in the air before finally hitting Leanora the beaver on the nose. She began to shiver and shake, before spinning around in circles. Then, the pile of clothes rose from the ground and disappeared into the spinning circle, which grew taller and taller until the top of it seemed to disappear up into the sky. When, at last, it became smaller and smaller and ceased to twist and spin at all, there in front of her once more stood her dear friend Leanora the Gypsy. Luckily, she was clothed, although her felt hat was missing and her grubby big toes could be seen protruding from her scruffy brown socks since, of course, she had no shoes on her feet.

"I thought you said the wand wouldn't work unless it had been enchanted by the elfin queen," said Rose Iris.

"Oh, it works for silly, easy spells like the one I have just used, but it will be useless against Gregoran's magic. As you have already seen, his spells are very strong," replied the old Gypsy. "Now, we must go and find Vilabria, the queen of the elves, and I know exactly where to find her."

Vilabria the Elfin Queen

Leanora lifted her little friend gently from the ground and placed her safely in her cardigan pocket. Then the old Gypsy picked up the two pieces of branch she had chewed from the boobar tree and pushed one up each of her cardigan sleeves. Rose Iris chose to stand up inside the pocket with her arms dangling over the top of it.

They travelled only a short distance along the edge of the stream before arriving at a forest. Leanora crept carefully amongst the trees and undergrowth until at last they reached a clearing. She knew this was where she would find the elfin kingdom. The leaves on the trees sparkled like emeralds and diamonds as the sun peeped gently through their branches, and the flowers shone brightly, like rubies and pearls. Hundreds of will-o-the-wisps twinkled and floated all around them, their high pitched, tinkling voices echoing amongst the trees. After walking for a short while they arrived at a beautiful garden, in the centre of which there glistened a small, silent pool of water. This was truly a magical kingdom.

Unusual looking people with tiny, pointed noses and large, pointed ears walked past them. They were slightly taller than Leanora, and very much slimmer. All wore clothes of different shades of green, and as they passed by the old Gypsy, everyone nodded and smiled before wishing her a very good day. Their children played amongst the trees and flowers, but as Leanora walked past them, they stopped playing and stared at the little human, because they had never seen such a peculiar thing before.

"Don't stare, it is very rude to stare," said the grown-ups to the children, when they saw the funny little creature who popped her head over the top of Leanora's pocket.

"What is it, Mother?" said one little boy.

"My dear, I think you have been fortunate to have seen Rose Iris," replied his mother. "I have told you about her brave adventures, and how she and the flea army saved all the country folk from the evil rock trolls," she continued. "Now stop staring or you will make the child think she is peculiar."

The old Gypsy walked towards the pool and stood at the water's edge. She stretched her arms as far as she could over the calm, clear water. Holding one of the wands she had made earlier in each hand she spoke these words.

"Vilabria, my gracious queen, I have one wish to ask.
Please enchant these wands, so we can complete our task.
We need to save a princess, the beautiful Mae Woo.
Without your help, I must confess, I know not what to do.
Her life is in great danger and her father lies adying.
We cannot leave them to their fate without our even trying.
The evil wizard Gregoran the princess hides from view,
And we must try to rescue her, then save her father too."

Leanora stopped chanting and waited patiently, for she knew the queen would not ignore her request. At first nothing happened. Then suddenly the water began to swirl like bath water as it runs down the plughole. First the circle disappeared into the calm water then it rose up towards the sky, before forming into a glistening fountain. Suddenly the beautiful elfin Queen Vilabria emerged from the water like a vision. She wore similar green clothes to all the other elves. Her hair was jet black and cascaded down to almost touch the glimmering water. Gliding slowly and gracefully towards the water's edge, she held out her arms in welcome to the old Gypsy.

"Leanora, how lucky we are to have you visit us today. We must have a party to celebrate your arrival." Her voice was soft and almost musical when she spoke.

Leanora bowed her head and curtsied before looking pleadingly into the queen's beautiful face. "Your Majesty, I regret we are unable to stay, for we must save Princess Mae Woo from Gregoran the wizard before the Emperor of China dies of a broken heart." Leanora replied. "I am very grateful for your kindness but please forgive my rudeness."

"Very well, I can understand that you and Rose Iris are in a hurry, so I will grant your wish and then I insist you come to visit us again soon," said Vilabria.

"Do you know me, Your Majesty?" said the little girl politely.

"Everyone knows about the little girl who saved the wind whistlers, rock doppies, earth crabbits and mud fairies from the rock trolls. I am honoured to meet you, my dear," Vilabria replied.

Rose Iris was shocked to hear that a beautiful elfin queen was honoured to meet her, but could find no suitable words in reply.

"Will you hold out your wands once more, so I am able to enchant them?" Vilabria smiled in a royal manner as she spoke.

"Yes, Your Majesty," Leanora immediately obeyed the queen's wishes and held the two pieces of chewed tree

VILABRIA

branch at arm's length towards Vilabria. Rose Iris was surprised to see that without speaking even one word the queen caused the wands to turn to gold. Then as quickly as they had turned to gold, they once more became just two parts of the same dull, brown branch that Leanora had chewed from the boobar tree.

"Now you must be on your way. I realise how urgent your mission is," said Vilabria. "Go safely with my blessing, and I hope you will soon return."

"May I request just one more thing from Your Majesty? And please may I whisper my wish into your ear?" asked the Gypsy.

"Of course," replied Vilabria, and she leaned towards Leanora to enable the old Gypsy to whisper a secret that nobody else could hear, not even Rose Iris.

The queen nodded in agreement to whatever Leanora had requested. "Now you must hurry away for it is beginning to get dark. I will send my will-o-the-wisps to light your way."

So, after saying goodbye to the elfin queen, they set out on their journey back towards Gregoran's castle. The elves gave them food and the will-o-the-wisps accompanied them to the edge of the forest, lighting their path as they went.

"What did you whisper into Queen Vilabria's ear?" asked Rose Iris.

"That, my dear, is a secret," replied her friend. "If I tell you what the secret is, it will no longer be a secret. Will it?"

"Of course, as usual, you are quite right," answered the little girl.

The Race to Find the Princess

When at last they arrived back at the old pram darkness had fallen, and since it was very cloudy there was no moon and there were no stars lighting the sky. Droodle had woken up and sat on the blanket chatting happily to a firefly, but when he saw the old Gypsy he shooed the firefly away and once more put on his important expression.

"I have been guarding the pram all the while you have been away," he smiled innocently, although even he knew he was fibbing.

"Oh dear," thought Leanora. "Now he will want to come with us," but she knew exactly how to make him stay behind. "Now, I insist that you accompany us on this terribly dangerous journey, from which you may never return," she said.

Droodle thought for a moment. He did not want to go somewhere from whence he may not return. He wanted to go on an adventure, but he wasn't that adventurous. Anyway, nobody was going to tell him what he must do.

"I think it would be much safer, err, I mean braver, if I stay here and guard your precious belongings," he said.

"Very well, if you insist," said the old Gypsy. The plan had worked. Leanora knew that Droodle would never do as he was told. Gently, the old Gypsy slid her fingers under the old blanket and slowly pulled out her magic mirror. As she and Rose Iris looked into it a cloud of smoke formed, then slowly disappeared to reveal a very sad vision. The Emperor of China was just a few days from death and preparations were being made to wish him a safe journey on his travels to the spirit world. Tears welled up in Leanora's eyes as she carefully replaced the mirror under the blanket, together with the smaller of the two wands.

"There is no time to sleep," said the old Gypsy. "We must leave right away."

They left Droodle some of the food the elves had given them before setting out again. So, with Rose Iris tucked in her pocket Leanora once more entered the secret door. Then she retraced her steps until they reached the trap door. The old Gypsy climbed through once more and stood in the passageway in the castle. She found her pile of clothes, which still lay on the floor in one of the rooms. First, she removed her cardigan, then she slid her many jumpers over her head before replacing it. Next, she slipped on her shoes, placed her hat on her head and the gold locket around her wrist.

Now they began their search for Princess Mae Woo. Leanora crept silently from each grey, stony room to the next, but the princess was nowhere to be seen. Then, in one of the rooms Rose Iris noticed a long, red curtain that hung from the ceiling to the floor. The curtain had gotten caught up on a doorknob.

"Look Leanora, I think there is a door behind that curtain," the little girl whispered.

The old Gypsy approached the curtain and carefully pulled it back, revealing a glass door. She gave a sudden gasp. "It's a portal," she whispered.

"What is a portal?" asked Rose Iris.

"A portal is a magic door. You simply have to enter it and

order it to take you somewhere, and it will immediately obey your command." Leanora placed her hand on the doorknob and turned it as she spoke. The door opened to reveal nothing but a white cloud of dust. The old Gypsy stepped into the cloud and ordered, "take us to Princess Mae Woo." Immediately the cloud disappeared, and they found themselves in what appeared to be a large cave. Pieces of beautiful silk clothing lay scattered about the floor of the cave. Then suddenly, as they looked about them, they became very afraid. It was not the grey walls or the flickering torches that frightened them. It was the gigantic, green dragon that stood on a pile of rocks, beneath an arch in the centre of the cave, and what was even more disturbing was that the dragon had seen them.

"Oh dear, I believe we are too late, and this dreadful dragon has already eaten Mae Woo," said Leanora. "These must be her clothes that are scattered about the cave." Quickly, she slid her hand up her sleeve and pulled out her new magic wand. Her hand was trembling as she pointed it towards the dragon.

"I hope this wand is going to work," she said. "After all I have only used it once to turn myself back from a beaver to a Gypsy. It will take very strong magic to kill a dragon."

"Oh no, please don't kill me," said a soft, tearful voice. "I am only a poor princess. A wicked wizard has taken me from my dear parents and turned me into this dreadful creature. He is keeping me prisoner in this miserable place. Please don't hurt me. I promise I would never hurt you." The poor creature looked more frightened of Leanora and Rose Iris than they were of her.

"Do not be afraid, Princess. I and my little friend here

THE DRAGON

have come to rescue you, then take you home to your mother and father." She lowered her magic wand. "I am a witch, but you need not be afraid of me, for I only use my magic for goodness. I like to travel in my human form, as a Gypsy. My little friend is also a human like yourself. Her name is Rose Iris." Leanora did not tell the dragon princess that her father was slowly wasting away for love of his daughter.

The dragon knew she could trust this kind person who was going to take her home to her father, for she had the most warm, gentle voice. "Will you be able to help me?" she asked.

Leanora did not reply. She lifted her magic wand and pointed it towards the dragon princess.

"Destardo, excabardo, zorabora Mae Woo," she chanted.

As before, a blue light left the end of her wand and hit the dragon on the nose. It began to shiver and shake. Then its front legs rose from the rock it stood on. Its back legs also floated up into the air, until it stood on the tip of its tail. Finally, it began to spin around and around. There in front of them was a giant, spinning ball of green dust. Then the scattered clothes rose from the ground and one after another they floated into the swirling circle. After a while, the spinning slowed, and the dust began to settle before it disappeared completely, and in its place stood the beautiful Princess Mae Woo. She still looked a little unsteady, dizzy and very pale, but after a short while a little colour returned to her cheeks and she felt much stronger. Black, shiny hair surrounded her pale, almost white skin, and she was dressed in the most glorious silk clothing. After throwing her arms about the old Gypsy's shoulders she began to sob.

"How can I ever thank you enough for saving me?" she cried. "If I ever see my dear father again, he will pay you with many chests of gold," she continued as she slowly released Leanora from her arms.

"Now, we came here to find you through a portal, so there must be another portal nearby. We must look for the new door and then we can use it to take you safely back to China and your loving parents," said Leanora. She ignored the princess's promise to make her rich.

It was a very large cave that they had to search, and it took a very long time to find the portal. It was hidden under a long grey curtain that seemed to disappear into the grey rocks.

As before, the portal was made of glass. Leanora slowly opened the door, and with Rose Iris safely in her pocket she clasped Mae Woo's hand tightly as they passed through the opening and into the cloud of white that floated silently on the other side.

"Take us to the Emperor of China," she commanded.

Immediately they found themselves in a beautiful garden. White statues lined the paths that stretched as far as the eye could see. Men and women, who were dressed very plainly in loose trousers and tops and wore hats that looked like cones because they were round and almost flat but went up to a point, were tending the plants and blossoming trees that filled the garden. The portal was hidden so well under a hanging wisteria tree that it would have been impossible to find had they not just travelled through it.

"We must remember where this door is," said Leanora, "for we will need to return through it to go back to the magical world."

"Oh, how wonderful," said a tiny, musical voice. "The princess has come back."

PRINCESS MAE WOO

From Leanora's pocket, Rose Iris looked in the direction of the voice and saw hiding amongst the blossom on the branch of a tree the prettiest bird she had ever seen. Then after seeing movement on a nearby branch, she saw a second identical bird. Both birds began to sing a most beautiful song.

"Leanora, please may I return to your hat?" said the little girl. "I find it hard to stand up in your pocket, and I cannot see so well from this position."

The old Gypsy gently lifted the little girl from her pocket and allowed her to climb from her finger onto her hat, which was not looking as beautiful as it usually did, since many of the berries had shrivelled and all the flowers were dead. Still, Rose Iris had the hatband to cling onto.

"Excuse me, I wonder if you would accompany us to the palace, and then guide us back to this place?" Leanora asked the birds for their help. "You see, we must return to this magical door in order to travel back to our own world, but the garden is so vast and the door so well hidden that we will never be able to find it again."

"Of course, we will help you," replied the birds.

"I am Leanora and this little human on my hat is called Rose Iris. You already know the princess."

"You may call me Rosie if you like," said the little girl. "My parents call me Rosie and so does my dear friend Bert the wood pigeon. My little brother just calls me Wosie because he cannot speak very well yet."

"Are you speaking to me?" said Princess Mae Woo.

"No, Your Highness, we are speaking to the birds," said the old Gypsy.

That was when Rose Iris realised that only Leanora and

herself could hear the birds talking. The princess did not have the gift of hearing and speaking with the animals.

"I can't wait to tell my parents all about you and your magic spells, and they will be amazed that you have a tiny human friend as a companion." said the princess.

"No, you must tell nobody about my little friend, or that I have the power to work magic," said Leanora. "For if you do you will be struck dumb and never be able to speak again."

Mae Woo was disappointed. She wanted to tell everyone about her rescuer's magic and thought her parents would be delighted to meet the little girl, but she did not want to be struck dumb and so she promised to keep their secret to herself.

Only Just in Time

The palace was as white as snow. It had many green tiled roofs, at different levels. Each roof curled upwards at all four corners and a golden dragon statue decorated each of them. A flight of very wide marble steps rose towards the entrance to the palace. Leanora lifted Rose Iris from her hat and hid her carefully beneath it. Guards dressed in colourful uniforms bowed very low as the princess and her friend approached. They did not see the little girl who hid silently under Leanora's hat, but she could see them through a tiny hole.

When they entered the palace a very important looking gentleman, dressed in long, colourful, silken robes approached them and bowed to the princess. He was tall and slim with a long white beard. As he hurried them through the rooms and corridors past ornate mirrors, and ornaments, Rose Iris peeped out and noticed his long white hair had been tightly pulled to the back of his neck and hung in a plait that reached almost down to his bottom.

"Why are you taking us to my parent's bedroom, ambassador?" asked the princess. "Surely they are in their living quarters at this time of day," she continued.

"I am afraid your father is so broken hearted that he took to his bed when you disappeared and has not risen since," replied the ambassador.

"Then hurry, we must see him as soon as possible," ordered the princess as she began to weep and sob aloud.

When at last they arrived at the emperor's bedroom, they

found it to be guarded, but as they approached the door the two guards who stood outside bowed to the princess and moved aside, allowing them to enter.

A very sad sight welcomed them when they had passed through the door. There lay the emperor, fast asleep. His wife, the empress, who was Mae Woo's mother, sat beside him. Tears streamed down her face before silently sliding from her chin, and finally soaking into the beautiful silk bedclothes. Everyone else in the room stood silent. When the ambassador hurried into the bedroom, followed by the princess and Leanora, everyone looked up to see what was causing such a commotion.

"Oh, my dear, beautiful daughter," cried the empress. "Maybe you have come just in time to save you poor father from taking his last breath."

Mae Woo rushed to the emperor's bedside, knelt down and gently took her father's hand in hers. She kissed him softly on his pale, white cheek.

Rose Iris secretly peeped out from under Leanora's hat as the old Gypsy approached the emperor's bedside. Nobody noticed the little girl, for all eyes were on Princess Mae Woo as she kissed and stroked her father's forehead. She gave a soft sob as his limp hand slipped from hers and flopped lifeless onto the bedclothes.

"Dear Father, do not leave us for I have returned and cannot bear to be without you. You will break my heart if you die."

Still her father lay silent, breathing so softly that he hardly breathed at all. Then suddenly, one finger on his left hand moved and his eyes slowly flickered before finally opening very slightly, then closing once more. All was silent except for the sobs of the princess and her mother. That was when the most wonderful thing happened. The emperor opened his eyes once again, only this time they stayed open and his lips formed into a smile. He had recognised his daughter and the sight of her had overjoyed him and given him the will to live. Slowly the colour returned to his face and he tried hard to sit up in his bed, but was not strong enough to do so, for he had not eaten for such a very long time.

"Please do not tire yourself, Father," said Mae Woo, "for now I am back with you and my dear mother I will never leave you again. May I introduce you to this wonderfully kind Gypsy lady, whose name is Leanora. She brought me back to the palace in time to save your life, and I know you will want to reward her greatly," she continued.

"Thank you for saving my daughter and bringing her home to us," said the emperor. He lifted his head with difficulty as he spoke in a weak, soft voice. "I will grant you anything you wish for if it is in my power to do so. Gold, diamonds, jade, anything you desire will be yours."

"I want very little, Your Emperorship," replied Leanora. "There is just one small gift I would ask for. In your garden you have many berries and flowers. Please could I have some to decorate my felt hat. It is usually very beautiful, you see, but I am afraid all the berries have shrivelled up and all the flowers have died. It has been such a very long time since I have been able to replace them."

"Are you sure that is all you wish for?" asked the emperor.

"Oh yes, thank you. There is nothing more I need, for I have everything anyone could wish for," replied the old Gypsy. "If Your Emperorship does not mind, I would like to leave now, since I have to return someone else safely back to her parents."

Rose Iris stopped looking out from under the hat for she was afraid someone may see her now that everyone had stopped staring at the emperor and his beautiful daughter.

"Of course, you must quickly find this other child and return her to her parents," said the empress. She had no idea that the little girl to whom Leanora referred was already hiding under the old Gypsy's hat. "The palace servants will give you fresh food for your journey," she continued.

Back to the Pram and Droodle

So, Leanora said goodbye to the emperor and empress. Princess Mae Woo accompanied her as she left the palace and walked back down the marble steps into the garden. Rose Iris returned to sit on top of the old Gypsy's hat, but she was very tired for she had not slept for such a long time. Her eyes kept closing and every now and then she would loosen her grip on the hatband as she struggled to stay awake.

On a tree just outside the palace, the two birds waited patiently. They were very excited to be helping the funny looking lady and the tiny little girl, who both had the gift of being able to speak to them and understand what they were saying.

Rose Iris tried hard to cling tightly to Leanora's hatband as the birds flew from tree to tree and guided them back towards the secret portal that was hidden under the wisteria. Then, all of a sudden, her hands lost their grip, and she came tumbling off the brim of the hat because she had fallen asleep.

Luckily for the tiny girl, Princess Mae Woo had noticed her falling and quickly stepped forward to catch her as she fell.

Rose Iris did not wake up, even when Mae Woo kissed the sleeping child and passed her carefully back to Leanora, who placed her safely in her pocket.

As they walked along the path decorated with white statues, Leanora replaced the berries and flowers on her felt hat. Then, when they arrived back at the portal, the old Gypsy and the princess said their goodbyes.

"I will never forget you, for you not only saved me from a terrible end, but you also saved my father's life," said Mae Woo. "Are you sure there is nothing I can give you as a reward for your kindness?"

"There is just a small thing," replied Leanora. "In your hair you have some beautiful glass flowers. Please could I have one as a keepsake? It will look beautiful on my felt hat."

The princess said nothing. She took a glass flower ornament from her hair and kissed it before passing it to the old Gypsy. It was attached to a long pin and so Leanora pushed the pin into her newly decorated hat. Then Mae Woo pulled another glass flower from her hair and she herself carefully pushed the pin into the hat.

Rose Iris did not wake up when Leanora opened the portal door and she had no memories of the journey back to the castle, but suddenly she was awoken by loud shouting. Standing up in Leanora's pocket she peeped secretly over the top and was amazed to see that Gregoran the wizard and Leanora were arguing. Also, in the room were the yabberwak and Petrina the rat.

"Destardo, excabardo, zorabora monkey," Gregoran uttered the magic words as he pointed his magical, long walking stick towards Leanora.

A green light flashed across the room from the end of the stick towards Leanora, but the old Gypsy was ready with her strong new wand.

"Ditsigo, waggertag, stop this spell," said Leanora, and the brightest blue light Rose Iris had ever seen shot from the end of the wand. As both magic spells crashed into each other they exploded, but Leanora's spell seemed to gobble up Gregoran's much weaker magic.

The horrible wizard stood amazed. Nobody had ever had a wand strong enough to be better than his walking stick. Once more he pointed it towards the Gypsy, but he had taken too long to think about what he would do next.

"Destardo, excabardo, zorabora goat," Leanora directed her wand towards the wizard again as she spoke.

The shining blue light once more whizzed toward Gregoran, only this time it walloped him hard on the nose. First, he shivered, then he shook. His pointed shoes rose from the ground and he began to spin around and around. He spun faster and faster until it made Rose Iris feel quite dizzy just watching him turn. At last, the spinning stopped, and the little girl gasped for there in front of her stood an old goat. Petrina the rat climbed onto the pile of wizard's clothes that lay on the floor in the centre of the room, and the yabberwak looked on in amazement. Gregoran was so shaken up by what had happened to him he was unable to speak a single word.

Leanora directed her wand towards the goat once more and spoke these words.

"You will stay in this form until you're less cruel,
And if you don't change, you'll turn into a mule."

Rose Iris settled down inside the cardigan pocket and drifted back into a deep sleep, and the old Gypsy continued her

GUESS WHO?

journey through the trap door, down the steps and finally out of the secret door that had been guarded by the negradon. The little girl remembered nothing of this journey for she had been sleeping deeply.

When Leanora arrived back at the old pram she found Droodle fast asleep. Carefully she lifted the limp, sleeping child from her pocket and placed her gently beside the naughty rock doppy. Then she began her journey back toward Rose Iris's home, pushing the old pram with the rattling pots and pans, and humming cheerfully as she went.

After a while Rose Iris awoke and sat up. She gave Droodle a shake and he grumbled until he saw Leanora's large very angry face looking down at him.

"Oh dear, I am afraid I have been so brave guarding the pram, that I was unable to stay awake any longer," he fibbed, when he realised that both the old Gypsy and Rose Iris had returned safely. "You have been so lucky to go on a great adventure, whilst I have been left behind doing the boring but brave job," he continued. Only we know that he was not telling the truth. He even fibbed to himself by thinking, "I would have liked to go on their adventure, but they wouldn't let me."

Rose Iris returned to sit on Leanora's freshly decorated hat and noticed that as well as fresh berries and flowers, there were some new decorations. They were two gleaming glass flowers that glistened in the sunlight. She remembered that Mae Woo had worn the ornaments in her hair. "How lucky," she thought for Leanora to have such a wonderful gift from the princess. She wished she had something to remind her of the time she had met a real Chinese princess.

They travelled until it began to get dark. Then Leanora lit

a small fire and all three sat on the grass and ate some of the delicious food that the emperor's servants had given to them. Rose Iris told Droodle about the terrible wizard, Petrina the witch, and finally Princess Mae Woo and the emperor.

"It's not at all fair," said the naughty rock doppy. "I had to miss all the fun and adventure, having to be brave and stay behind and I so much wanted to have an amazing adventure. I could have asked the emperor for a reward but now I have nothing to prove how brave I have been." Then he yawned loudly, before lying down on the grass and falling fast asleep.

Soon afterwards Leanora took off her hat and laid it on the grass beside her. Then she fell into a deep sleep. Rose Iris wasn't tired, for she had slept in Leanora's pocket for quite some time. So, she lay awake staring up at the stars and wondering where her friends the moonbeams were. She wondered if they were floating down the stream on a beautiful leaf boat, like they were the night she had met them. She also thought about her dear friend Ilani and all the other mud fairies that had accompanied her on her first adventure. She was too excited to sleep but then suddenly she heard a familiar sound. A tick, tick, ticking sound which made her feel very sleepy, and before long she lay dreaming peacefully on top of Leanora's hat.

Cornelius Cornstalk

They set out early the following morning. Leanora was beginning to worry that too much time had passed since she and Rose Iris left the park to try to save Princess Mae Woo from the wicked wizard, and the little girl's parents may be looking for her. As usual, time was passing much faster in the magical world, but they still had some way to travel before they would arrive back at the park from whence their journey had begun.

As the old Gypsy pushed her pram along a lane, she hummed happily, but as they passed a field of corn she stopped suddenly when she heard voices. She could tell by the tone of one of the voices that somebody was in distress.

"I be not liking to frighten you away, cos you be my friends," said a rather sad voice, "but farmer Brown says he be going to throw me on the compost heap if I don't scare you off, cos I be good for nothing. Please will you leave me alone and stop eating the corn in my field?" he continued.

Leanora pushed her old pram along a pathway that the farmer had made between the corn. The pots and pans made a terrible din, as they clashed and clattered against one another whenever the pram went over a large bump, which was most of the time. Then Rose Iris saw what was causing the commotion. It was a very smart looking scarecrow. On his left shoulder sat a large black crow, and a second crow was about to land on his right shoulder.

"Whatever is the matter, Cornelius?" asked Leanora.

"It's a terrible thing that be going to happen to me,"

replied the scarecrow. "Farmer Brown says I be good for nothing, cos I cannot frighten off the crows, and he be going to throw me on the compost heap. I be in a terrible mess, cos I like my friends and cannot scare them away, so they keep eating the corn and making my master angry."

"If your friends don't care about farmer Brown throwing you onto the compost heap because you are too kind and won't scare them away, then they are not really your friends at all," said Rose Iris angrily.

Leanora said nothing, although she was very impressed with the little girl's wisdom.

"No matter how you hate to frighten the crows, you must do so. For if they cared as much about you as they do about themselves, they would stop tormenting you, and get their corn from some other scarecrow's cornfield," Rose Iris continued.

"No, I be not wanting to scare anybody. I be liking my friends too much, and I don't know how to do it anyway," said Cornelius.

"Well, you will have to learn," ordered the little girl. "Just shout BOO as loud as you can. Then pull a really scary face and that will frighten them away from your cornfield."

Cornelius took a deep breath and puffed out his chest, "Boo," he whispered. Then he pulled what he thought was a most scary face, but it was impossible for him to look nasty because he was much too kind.

"Ha, ha, ha," joked the crows, "you couldn't scare a lady-bird off a poppy leaf. You couldn't even frighten a grasshopper off a blade of grass or a fly of a cowpat," they continued, as they jumped up and down on Cornelius's shoulders in fits of laughter.

CORNELIUS CORNSTALK

"Stop that right now," Rose Iris spoke in a very bossy manner. "Do you not realise, that if farmer Brown gets rid of poor Cornelius, he will bring another scarecrow into this field? One who may be very scary indeed."

The two crows looked at each other for a while, then started to giggle before bursting out in loud fits of laughter. "We ain't afraid of no scarecrow, nor a tiny little human being like you," said one of them, as he carried on rolling about and chuckling with laughter.

"No, maybe not, but I wonder if, when farmer Brown realises that you are not afraid of scarecrows, he will decide to bring his big gun into this field and shoot you. Will you be afraid then?" The little girl pulled a scary face as she spoke. "Will you be afraid to know that he will take you home and ask Mrs. Brown to cook you for dinner? First, she will cut off your heads, before plucking out your beautiful feathers. She will chop you up and put you into some pastry to make a pie. Finally, you will go into a very hot oven to cook."

Leanora watched on but said nothing. She could not believe that the little girl was so clever. Rose Iris had used the exact words that she would have used herself.

The two crows looked at each other once more, only this time the laughter had gone from their eyes, and in its place, there was a look of horror. Then one of them flew to sit beside the other on Cornelius's right shoulder. They whispered to each other secretly for some time before one of them spoke.

"Well, I think we must be going now," he said.

"We may pop in to see you if we are passing by, Cornelius," said his friend. Although they had already decided that they would never pass that way again.

As they flew over her head Leanora felt a soft plop on her left shoulder. "Wicked, dirty little creatures," she shouted after the crows when she saw that one of them had pooped on her.

As Leanora wiped the poop off, Droodle rolled about with laughter.

"Now you know how awful it was for me getting covered in ogre spit," he laughed.

"Imagine how wonderful it will be from now on. You will no longer have to worry about farmer Brown putting you on the compost heap," said Leanora, whilst completely ignoring the rock doppy's cheeky remark. "Everything in your life will make you happy from now on." The old Gypsy was so pleased that Cornelius was not going on the compost heap, and she was extremely pleased that Rose Iris was becoming so clever and wise.

"Well not really, cos I be in love with someone who doesn't even know how I is feeling," said Cornelius. "I be wanting to ask Lavinia Lovage to the full-moon ball, but her be so butiful all the other scarecrows will ask her. I isn't very handsome you see, so I be not brave enough to ask her to go with me. One day, I be wanting to marry her, but she probably will never even notice me."

"It's not hard to be brave," said Droodle. "I am very brave indeed. I have already done amazingly brave things, but I will not boast about myself. Ouch," he yelled as he bit his tongue because he was fibbing again.

"I think you are extremely handsome," said Rose Iris. "What is more, you are a very nice person and that is much more important. If you asked me to go to the full-moon ball I would love to come at any other time, but at this moment I must hurry back to the human world. Of course, Lavinia will not know how you feel about her if you are too shy to speak to her. Please promise me that you will ask her to go with you to the ball."

"Do you really think her may like me?" said Cornelius. "Suddenly I be feeling very brave, and tonight when all the scarecrows leave their posts, I promise I is going to ask my butiful Lavinia to be kind enough to accompany me to the full-moon ball."

"We are pleased to hear that, but now we must be on our way," said Leanora. So, they said their goodbyes and the old Gypsy retraced her steps to the lane and continued her journey back towards the park, once more pushing her old pram and humming a merry tune. Droodle had by then fallen asleep and Rose Iris sat on top of the old Gypsy's hat. By now she knew all the tunes that Leanora hummed and so she joined in with the humming.

Lavinia Lovage

As they continued along the lane, they passed a field of sweetcorn and they heard someone sobbing. From the top of Leanora's hat Rose Iris was able to see over the sweetcorn and was surprised to notice only a short distance away another scarecrow.

"Who is that crying?" said the old Gypsy, whose eyes could not see over the tall stalks of sweetcorn.

"I don't believe it. It is another scarecrow that is crying, only this time it is a lady. I had no idea that scarecrows all seem to be terribly unhappy," said the little girl. "Can we see if we can help her, Leanora?"

The old Gypsy put the brake on the pram in which Droodle was once again sleeping and left it in the lane whilst she walked into the field with the little girl still sat on her hat. The scarecrow continued to cry loudly. Her sore, red eyes were filled with teardrops.

"Whatever is the matter, Lavinia?" asked Leanora. "Why are you so sad?"

"Well, it's just that all the scarecrows keep asking me to go to the full-moon ball with them," Lavinia replied sadly.

"Surely that is a good thing. You will be able to choose the most handsome and kindest scarecrow to take you to the ball," said Rose Iris.

"That's just the problem," replied Lavinia. "The most handsome and kindest person has not asked me to go with him. My heart is breaking because I am sure he will ask another more presentable scarecrow to go. Someone like

Belinda Broadbean or Chicory Chickpea. They are always dressed much more elegantly than I am, and neither of them has a big wide mouth like I do."

"Who is this handsome fellow?" asked Leanora. "Is it Cornelius Cornstalk?"

"Why yes. How did you guess?" By now the scarecrow had stopped sobbing and was pleased that someone cared about how unhappy she was.

"Cornelius must be the most handsome gentleman hereabout and he is certainly the kindest," said Rose Iris. "I will tell you a secret and you must not tell a soul otherwise the secret won't be a secret anymore. Leanora, will you please put me on Lavinia's shoulder?"

Leanora did as she was asked, and Rose Iris whispered in Lavinia's ear. "Cornelius is deeply in love with you. He wants to take you to the full-moon ball but has not had the courage to ask you to go with him. He thinks he is not as handsome as all the other gentleman scarecrows," she continued, "but he has promised to ask you tonight."

"What about Belinda Broadbean and Chicory Chickpea?" said Lavinia. "I know they are both waiting for him to ask them to accompany him to the ball. Surely he will not ask me if he can take one of them. They are much more elegantly dressed than me. My dress is too short, and you have no idea how embarrassing it is to always have your knickers showing and your stockings hanging down around your ankles," she began to cry again.

"Don't cry, Lavinia," said Leanora. "Cornelius loves you just as you are, but if you like I will pull up your stockings and tuck them under your knicker-legs, and I will get a beautiful mauve ribbon from my pram and tie it around your

LAVINIA LOVAGE

pretty hat. It will match perfectly. Unfortunately, I cannot do anything about your dress being too short, but it is a very pretty dress, and your knickers are actually quite nice."

A very broad smile crossed Lavinia's lovely face as she waved goodbye to Leanora and Rose Iris.

The Four Wonderful Gifts

Eventually they arrived back at the park opposite Rose Iris's house. The little girl sat on the old felt hat thinking it was sad that her adventure was almost over, and Droodle lay sleeping soundly in the pram. The sky became very cloudy and there were a few light showers. Although the rain was not heavy enough to make Leanora and Rose Iris very wet, it did leave a few muddy puddles along their path. The old Gypsy's shoes let in the water as she stepped through one shallow puddle after another. Her socks became soaking wet as the water seeped in through the holes in her shoes, then it squelched back out again each time she put her foot on the ground between the puddles.

Suddenly there was an awful screeching sound and a flapping of wings. Then, something really terrible happened. A large bird swooped down and snatched Leanora's hat straight off her head, taking quite a few strands of hair with it. What was even more terrible was that Rose Iris was still on the hat. She clung tightly to the hatband as the bird soared up into the air. Large feet clenched the hat tightly. Then the little girl heard a familiar voice.

"Urry up, Jed, we ain't got all day," it squawked.

It was one of the two horrible magpies that had held her and her dear mud fairy friend Ilani captive under two stones in her first adventure. They had stolen her watch and wanted her grandmother's locket, but she had refused to give it to them. Now they had stolen Leanora's freshly decorated hat.

"Did yer get it, Mort?" another familiar voice screeched.

"Yea, course I did, Jed, but there's one of them 'orrible little fings on it." As he spoke, he gave the hat a shake, hoping the little girl would fall off.

"Well let me 'ave it then," screamed Jed. "Is the two shiny fings still on it too?"

"Yea, they are, but you ain't 'avin' 'em, cos I want 'em both. I got 'em so they're mine," replied Mort.

The old Gypsy watched helplessly as they began to fight in the air. They were too high for her magic to reach them. Then Mort gave a loud screech as the point of one of the glass pins that Mae Woo had given Leanora stuck into his toe.

"Ouch, the stupid 'ats got some spikey fings in it," he complained. In a panic they both let go of the hat and it fell down towards the ground. Rose Iris lost her grip on the hatband and fell with a plop into a dirty puddle, followed by the hat. The two birds flew off arguing as they usually did.

"It's your fault we ain't got no precious fings," squawked Mort.

"No, it ain't. Trouble is you want to keep all the good stuff for yourself," screeched his companion.

They continued to disagree as they disappeared into the distance.

Leanora ran as quickly as she could to rescue Rose Iris from the puddle, but it was already too late. The hat had landed upside down and the little girl was underneath it. She removed the hat from the puddle and was very relieved to see that Rose Iris was stood shoulder deep in the water. Luckily, it was not deep enough to drown her. The old Gypsy lifted the little girl, who was soaking wet and covered in mud from the puddle and held her in the palm of her hand.

"Now, although it was a little scary for me," said Leanora "and even more frightening for you, those two silly magpies have given me an idea. There was only enough magic potion to make you small and none left to make you grow big again, so I have been wondering how to return you to your parents, since there has been no heavy rain. Now Mort and Jed have helped me without realising it. Since you are soaking wet after falling into the puddle, I will be able to use my usual spell to enable you to grow to your normal size again." She took the little girl's golden locket from where she had kept it safely wrapped around her wrist and opened it to reveal the enchanted stones. Then she placed it in the palm of her hand beside Rose Iris. "You must touch the stones, then I will work my spell," she continued.

The little girl reached forward and touched the stones. "I'm ready," she said. "Please will you promise that you will not disappear when I am big again."

"Yes, I promise," said the old Gypsy, "for I have something very exciting to tell you, and some important advice to give you." Then she began to repeat her special shrinking and growing spell several times.

"Delgora, delgora, esparto, ventura
Malafont, gorgana alamantura."

Gradually Rose Iris began to get bigger and bigger. Leanora quickly placed her on the ground, which was just as well or she would have broken the old Gypsy's wrist, since she was becoming so heavy. When she at last reached her normal human size, she stopped growing. The most amazing thing was that her dear friend had not gone away or disappeared as she had on her previous adventures. Although they had spent many days in the magical world looking for and saving Princess Mae Woo, hardly any time at all had passed in the human world. She was surprised to see that still none of her friends had arrived at the park.

"I have four wonderful gifts for you," said Leanora. She reached under the blanket in the old pram and pulled out the smaller of the two wands that she had made when she was a beaver. "This is for you," she said. Then she slid her hand back under the blanket and when she pulled it out again she was holding her red book of spells. "This is also a gift to you," she continued.

"I am very grateful for your gifts but as you have told me I am unable to work magic yet," said Rose Iris.

"Now I am able to tell you the secret that I whispered into the elfin queen's ear," said the old Gypsy. "I asked Vilabria if you were ready to become an apprentice witch and would she bestow on you the gift of magic, and she was happy to agree with my request. You must only use this wonderful gift for good or the elves will take it away from you. You have already used magic once, even before your gift was given to you. When you returned from the world of ogres and got stuck between the rocks you used magic to ask them to open. It was not my magic but yours that helped you to free yourself."

"I'll never waste my gift by doing bad, unkind things, Leanora. Does that mean I will be able to see you, Ilani and all my other friends whenever I wish?" asked the little girl.

"No, not immediately, but eventually once you have learnt most of the spells in the red book you will become a fully qualified witch," Leanora replied. "I hope that when we meet again you will not need my help to cross over from one world to another, and neither will you need to become small again."

All this time Droodle had been sleeping peacefully in the old pram and even when the old Gypsy had removed the wand and spell book from under the blanket he had not stirred.

"Shall we wake Droodle so I can say goodbye?" asked Rose Iris.

"That would not be a good thing to do," said Leanora. "He will probably throw another tantrum if he knows you have become an apprentice witch. He will sulk if he knows you have been given gifts and he hasn't."

"Will you tell Ilani and the other mud fairies that soon I will be able to visit them whenever I choose?" said the little girl.

"Certainly I will, but how soon you are able to travel from the human world to the magical world will depend on how hard you work to learn your spells," replied Leanora. "Now I am afraid that you must return home before your parents become worried." As she spoke the old Gypsy clasped her arms around Rose Iris. "I can't wait until we can go on adventures together and you can stay human sized. We will be able to sit together beside my fires with a nice mug of tea, and chat for hours. I will ask my friend Dolly for an extra mug next time I visit the farm. Goodbye, dear friend." She gave the little girl one last squeeze and kissed her on the forehead as she spoke.

"Cheerio for now, Leanora. I am sure I will see you again very soon, for I mean to work very hard on my spells," said the little girl as she began to walk away.

"Have you not noticed that I have given you only three

gifts and I said there were four? There is one more that you deserve," said Leanora. She reached up to her old felt hat, which had become very wet but was drying nicely in the sunshine, and pulled out one of Princess May Woo's glass ornaments. "This is for you," she said.

"You can't give me that," said the little girl. "It is yours."

"Well, if I have to worry about Mort and Jed trying to steal it all the time it will be safer with you," replied Leanora.

As Rose Iris walked back to her home and Leanora walked in the opposite direction they both turned occasionally to wave to each other, until at last they had both disappeared from each other's sight.

When Rose Iris entered her house through the open kitchen door, she hoped her mother would not notice the wand and red book which she carried, or the glistening glass ornament she had threaded through her dress. She did not want to fib, and she knew there was only one person who would believe her story and that was her best friend. Well, her mother didn't see the book and wand, but she did give Rose Iris a good telling off because her clothes were all wet and muddy from the dirty puddle that she had fallen into when the naughty magpies had dropped her. She didn't hear her mother's complaints though, for her thoughts were elsewhere as she rushed straight upstairs and picked up Daisy, her rag doll. Then, she ran out of the back door and down to the bottom of the garden. She could not wait to start practising her spells.

From that time on she hardly went to the park, but instead would run straight to the bottom of the garden whenever she got home from school and would also spend all her spare time at weekends learning her spells. Unfortu-

ROSE IRIS

nately, nothing magical had happened, until one day she was trying to work magic to make a ladybird speak. She pointed her wand toward the little creature and read these magic words very carefully from the spell book.

"Dipsy, dopsy, diddledy dee,
I wish that you could speak to me."

She waited with the wand held in the air for a few moments, but nothing happened. Disappointed, she lowered the wand and accidentally hit Daisy on her head as she sat silently by her feet.

"Oh! Poor Daisy, I am sorry," said the little girl.

"That's alright, you didn't mean to hurt me," the rag doll replied in a quiet, gentle voice.

Rose Iris was so excited, for she had worked her first magic spell. After that day, her magic grew stronger and stronger until she became as good and almost as wise a witch as Leanora. She travelled back and forth between the human world and many other parallel worlds whenever she pleased and came to know all the creatures and fairy folk in those worlds just like the old Gypsy.

She told her best schoolfriend about all her wonderful adventures, and when her friend grew old, she too told her own granddaughters Sian, Natasha and Lana all about her dearest friend, Rose Iris, and her many travels and adventures with Leanora the Gypsy, who, I must remind you, also happened to be a witch.

The End
Or Maybe a New Beginning